Drama High, Vol. 1

THE FIGHT

Drama High, Vol. 1
THE FIGHT

L. Divine

Dafina Books for Young Readers
KENSINGTON PUBLISHING CORP.
http://www.kensingtonbooks.com

DAFINA BOOKS are published by

Kensington Publishing Corp.
850 Third Avenue
New York, NY 10022

All Kensington titles, imprints and distributed lines are available at special quantity discounts for bulk purchases for sales promotion, premiums, fund-raising, educational or institutional use.

Special book excerpts or customized printings can also be created to fit specific needs. For details, write or phone the office of the Kensington Special Sales Manager: Kensington Publishing Corp., 850 Third Avenue, New York, NY 10022. Attn: Special Sales Department. Phone: 1-800-221-2647.

Dafina Books and the Dafina logo Reg. U.S. Pat. & TM Off.

ISBN 0-7582-1633-5

First Trade Paperback Printing: October 2006
10 9 8 7 6 5 4 3 2 1

Printed in the United States of America

Acknowledgments

To Osun, thank you for your blessings. To my ancestors, thank you for your guidance. To my children, thank you for showing me what true love can create. To my mother, thank you for your undying faith. To my family and friends, thank you for being my village. To Rebecca Stewart and company, thank you for helping to bring my creations into reality a little sooner. To my students, thank you for your inspiration. To my audience, thank you for your support. To Simply Wholesome, Eso Won Books, and Forty-Second Street Elementary School, thank you for loving "Drama High" from the start. To my agent, Jenoyne Adams, thank you for being the best advocate an author can have. And, to my editor, Stacey Barney, thank you for turning my book into a novel and my series into a journey.

Prologue

It's the first day of school, and I'm standing in South Bay High's Main Hall. The air is thick with the smell of fresh paint. I think I'm alone, but then I see Nellie and Mickey are there and yelling at me; then suddenly, there are students all around us joining Nellie and Mickey in chanting, "Jayd, whip her ass!"

I turn to my opponent. She and I are in the middle of the frenzied students, circling each other like gladiators. I'm ready, I think. I take off my backpack and hand it to Nellie. When I do, my charm bag falls out, and I notice the writing on it. I can't make out what it says, but I know it's Mama's handwriting, and then I can hear her in my head telling me, "If you'd done your assignment like I told you to, you'd be able to fix this mess on your own. Now, you're going to have to fight your way out of it."

Before I can think about what it means, my sparring partner moves in close and slaps me across my face. There's an explosion of oohs and oh-no-she-didn'ts from the crowd. They're all looking at me now, wondering what I'll do. I won't lie; the blow hurts. I grab the right side of my face and look daggers at her, wishing she'd burst into flames. I taste blood and tears on my tongue as the crowd gets louder. I'm breathing hard now, and she's staring me down, daring me to retaliate. Her eyes tell me she doesn't think I will, but she's wrong. I take my time though, slipping off my gold hoop earrings and handing them to Nellie as well. I consider my opponent once more. Then I attack, reaching out with a slap of my own. She wraps her arm around my waist, pulling me to her. Entangled, we fall to the ground.

The crowd continues to egg me on. "Whip her ass, Jayd. Whip Misty's ass!" they say. I'm fighting Misty? I get up off the ground, where I've pinned her down, and look at her again. But nowhere in this girl crumpled on the floor, holding her face and side in pain, do I see Misty.

"It's over. Misty gives up," Mickey announces to the crowd. I look at Mickey confused.

This girl I'm fighting isn't Misty, I think. Then KJ reaches out from the crowd, grabbing me by the hand. He begins to lead me away, but I pull back to look once more at the girl who I saw so clearly just a minute before, but who now has no face, before taking KJ's hand and leaving the scene of the fight.

"Jayd, get up. You gone be late for work," my mom yells from her bed, snapping me out of my dream. It's early in the morning and I'm stretched out across my mom's sofa—my bed during the weekends and holidays that I spend with her. I sit up to find it's already hot as hell. I want to think about my dream. I try to remember the details, but they're already fading. Frustrated, I get up to wash my face and prepare for the day. The last two days of summer are waiting for me; no time to waste dreaming about drama. I know there's plenty of drama in the real world.

~ 1 ~
The Breakup

"Make me wanna holler/
The way they do my life"

—MARVIN GAYE

I haven't talked to my man, KJ, in two days. I know some-thing's up. That's probably why I had that weird dream last night. I'm still mad at him and Misty, my former best friend, for trying to hook up my first time doing it. So, I really don't want to talk to Misty at all, but KJ's a different story.

"Jayd, go ahead and take a twenty-minute while it's slow," Shahid says.

I love working at Simply Wholesome. It's way better than working at a fast-food restaurant like other kids my age. It's the only health-food store and restaurant I know of that's both Black owned—Shahid's the man—and supported. My uncle Bryan is so proud of me working here, him being both the Black revolutionary and vegetarian of the family. He loves it when I bring home free eats.

I walk outside to enjoy my break and look at the beautiful row of homes and Black folks in shiny cars. It's a perfect, sunny L.A. day, smog and all. I don't feel like snacking, not even my favorite spinach patties, so I take the opportunity to see why my man's tripping.

It's times like this I'm glad I splurged on a cell phone. It cost damn-near a whole paycheck, but I was tired of being the only person I knew without one.

I try to get a signal on my cell, but they're hard to pick up over here. I don't know if it's because we're so close to Kenneth Hahn Park, notorious for dropping calls, or because there are no cell wires near the oil wells on Stocker. Whatever it is, I'm lucky to get a signal at all.

What's up? Yes, you've reached him. KJ, The Man. Leave a message and maybe I'll get back.

Damn. It's his voice mail again. I've been calling him all weekend and I refuse to leave a message. He knows it's me.

I hang up the phone, pissed at his ass. Why is he avoiding me? I thought he was over last week's drama. Misty's probably told him all about me telling her off after she tried to pimp me out to him on our last date. I heard Maisha's back in town. He better not be with that heffa.

"Don't slip up and get caught, 'cause I'm coming for that number-one spot." I love that I can download Ludacris to my ring tone.

KJ's name pops up on my screen as the song plays. It's about time that fool called me back.

"Hello," I say, trying to sound both upset and sexy at the same time.

"What's up, Jayd?" He sounds cool as a cucumber, like he hasn't been avoiding me all weekend.

"You tell me. You the one not returning calls. Is there something you want to tell me?" I say.

Instead of apologizing or even responding, KJ only takes a deep breath and lets out a long sigh. It sounds like he's moving from one place to another.

"KJ, where are you?"

"Do you really want to know?" Now he sounds angry.

"What the hell is that suppose to mean?" I ask. I'm starting to feel sick to my stomach. This usually happens when something big is about to go down.

"Well, actually, I've been kinda kickin' it with someone else lately."

Now I know I'm going to be sick. "What the hell you mean by 'kickin' it,' KJ?!" I scream into the phone. People hangin' outside the restaurant are staring at me. I know this is so ghetto, but this fool's got me hot.

"What difference does it make, Jayd? I'm kickin' it with her the way I can't with you."

"What's that suppose to mean? We've only been together for a couple of months, KJ. How you gone give up on our relationship just like that?" Tears are streaming down my face, which I'm sure has turned red. Sarah, one of my coworkers, comes out to hand me a box of tissues from the store; when she goes back inside, she closes the door behind her.

As I blow my nose hard into the phone, I hear KJ telling someone to be quiet. Then I hear a door close in the background. My blood is boiling. Something told me he was with that heffa Maisha, or some other heffa. Just because I won't have sex with him? I don't believe this.

"Who was that, KJ?"

"Look, Jayd, I can't talk to you right now," he says. He still sounds cool. He's playing with me. "I'm kinda in the middle of something."

"Some*thing* or some*one*?" I ask. I'm getting angrier with every second that goes by.

"You know what, Jayd?" he says, sounding upset. "I ain't got time for this. I got to go tend to my company."

"What are you telling me, that you got another woman? What the hell? I thought you said you were in love with me?"

"I was, but you didn't do nothing to keep the love there, Jayd. And I got other females who are willing to show me how much they care."

I can't believe what I'm hearing. This fool is way too full of himself for me.

"Are you serious, KJ? Because those other females gave you some ass you think they love you more than I do?!" I shout, forgetting where I'm at. Customers are all over the place rushing in and out of Simply Wholesome and to their cars, but it doesn't matter; I'm about to go off.

"KJ, do you hear me talking to you? Answer me! Do you think I love you less because I won't give up the cookies?!" I say. Now I'm screaming at the top of my lungs. I wonder if these people even know what the hell cookies are.

"Jayd, you're being a little melodramatic for me. You had to see this coming."

I hear him sigh and then his other line clicks. It's probably one of his other broads on the line.

"How could I have seen this coming? Just last week you were telling me you loved me and you were willing to wait. What the hell? A week is waiting?" I can't believe this jerk is breaking up with me because I won't give it up to him. I should have Mama put a curse on him.

"Jayd, I can't do this right now. You get the message." And just like that, he hangs up.

How am I supposed to go back to work now? This fool just broke up with me over the phone. This fool that I love. I would call my mom, but it's Sunday and she's at church right up Slauson. I would ask her to pick me up, but I don't get off until four P.M. and it's only noon now.

"Jayd, break's over!" Shahid yells to me. He doesn't see the tears behind my sunshades. I wish I had time to call Mama. She'd know what to do. Maybe she can give KJ a wart on his forehead or something. I can't wait to get off work.

The bus ride home takes longer than usual. Maybe because my mind is on the fact that this morning I had a man and now I don't. When was he going to tell me? Tuesday, at school? Great way to start a new year.

As the bus rolls down LaBrea, the scenery quickly changes from rolling hills and beautiful homes to apartment buildings and liquor stores. Every time I leave work I feel like I'm Dorothy leaving Oz, but in a hood sort of way. As we approach Baldwin Hills, I look out of the bus window, wishing I could stop at Eso Won, my favorite bookstore and the only place Mama can find her special interest books. But, I can't. I'm too exhausted. I just want to go home and chill out.

There's tagging on the walls of businesses and bus stops with the different gang initials as we get closer to Inglewood. I remember I used to call myself a tagger in junior high. My tag name was "Lyttle." I can't really draw or even write fancy or nothing like that. But neither can half these fools out here.

Every now and again though I'll see some real hot tag displayed on an overpass or on the side of a bus that'll just take my breath away. Honestly, sometimes the tag art is better than whatever was there before it. But, that thug stuff has got to stop. That ain't art. That's just something somebody threw up to be rude. Tagging is about making a statement, not about being rude.

KJ's lucky I ain't the girl they used to call "Lyttle" no more. Otherwise, he and whatever hoodrat he's running with now would be in some serious pain. I used to fight boys and girls alike, at the drop of a dime. Fighting used to be my favorite pastime. Not because I liked it, but because I was good at it. Girls used to think that just because I'm pretty, I can't fight. They didn't know I was raised with a bunch of rough dudes and I could basically kick anybody's ass.

I didn't have any problems with gangs or people trying to jack me until my mom moved to Inglewood. I swear it seems like every time I go outside around here I'm either seeing some shit go down or I just missed it. I'm not saying anything's wrong with Inglewood. I just wish my mom lived on the other side by the Avenues and not over here in the hood. My mom's car gets broken in to so much, she doesn't even bother putting a new radio in it. Instead she makes do with her boom box on the car's floor or on my lap if I'm sitting in the passenger's seat.

When I get to my mom's house she's lying in her usual spot on the couch.

"Hey, girl. How was work?" my mom asks, all sleepy-like. Like most people on a hot Sunday afternoon, she was asleep before I walked in.

My mom's apartment is quiet, but hot. It gets so hot in this little place, sometimes I can't stand it. It's a one-bedroom, one-bathroom apartment with a little balcony right off the dining room. The kitchen, dining room, and living room all flow into one big room. My mom has excellent taste. She shops at spots like Pier 1 Imports and Cost Plus off Santa Monica Boulevard, so she has some real cute stuff.

Her house is in all natural tones. Her couch is beige accented with plush white-and-tan pillows and a bright, multi-colored throw that looks so pretty against her mahogany skin.

Lynn Marie Williams, aka my mom, is a fine little thing, to hear her men tell it. She's thirty-five, very petite, only five foot one inches, and only 120 pounds—most of that is up top—with long, black hair and bright green eyes, just like Mama's. Mama and my mom share the first name Lynn because when Mama first saw her daughter, it was like looking into a mirror. My mom can't say that about me though. If it weren't for our big breasts, we would look nothing alike.

I can still feel the knot in my throat from all the crying I did earlier. I don't feel like talking to my mom about KJ because she just wouldn't understand. She never has men problems. Ever.

"Jayd, why you standing there daydreaming? Don't you have packing to do? Don't forget you going back to Mama's tomorrow. Can't be until the afternoon though. The plumber's supposed to be coming in the morning to fix that leak in the bathroom."

"Mom, tomorrow's Labor Day, the day folks in this country don't work. Do you really think the same plumber who was supposed to show up a week ago is gone show up to work on a holiday?"

"Yes, because I went down there and talked to that wench myself and told her if that sink wasn't fixed by Monday morning, I would call the water company and report the leak."

That wench would be the manager, Ms. Bell. She acts like she's from the same place her name rhymes with. As I walk across the living room into the kitchen to get a glass of water, I notice my mom's been drinking some Alizé. No wonder she's in such a chill mood.

I walk out the kitchen through the dining room and onto the patio. My mom hears the patio door open and takes it as a reason to ask me her favorite question.

"When you gone get around to cleaning off that patio, Jayd?"

"When hell freezes over," I mumble under my breath. She's got to be joking if she thinks I'm gonna clean this mess for her. There's stuff out here from when she first moved here.

"What did you say?" my mom asks as she shifts from one side of the couch to the other to look at me.

"When I get some time, Mom. That's all I said."

I use one of her old suitcases as a chair and look out at the cement wall separating our driveway from the apartment next door. The eight-unit building is old as dirt, but usually well maintained. My mom moved here after she and my dad broke up a little over fourteen years ago. My dad still lives in the same house he lived in with my mom in Lynwood, a little city in between Compton and Watts. After they split up, my dad left her with nothing—no house, no money. Nothing. She left that house with what she had on and never looked back.

Just like KJ, my dad thinks he's the greatest gift to women. He's a good-looking man—tall, bright yellow skin, with a short-cropped afro, and a very charming personality. But, he's a dog—also just like KJ.

I can't stay in this cramped apartment with all this on my mind. I don't feel any better about KJ or Misty. When I need to get out, I take a walk to the liquor store.

I change out of my work clothes in the bathroom, putting on some Guess shorts and a Baby Phat tank top and some flip-flops from Target. I catch my reflection in the mirror and see I need to braid my hair tonight. Until then, a scarf will have to do.

I yell to my mom that I'm going for a walk and ask if she needs anything. She's still on the couch drifting in and out of sleep.

"Yes, Jayd. Could you please get me some Lay's chips and some sour cream?" she mumbles. "I feel like eating some onion dip."

"What kinda Lay's you want? Those new ones with the cheddar cheese are slammin'."

"No, Jayd, all that new stuff is for y'all youngsters. Just get me the kind in the yellow bag—plain."

"All right, but when I come back with my bag don't say nothing."

"Whatever, Jayd. Oh, and can you bring some French's onion soup mix too?" my mom asks, still in the same position.

"So basically, you have nothing in the house to make what you want and you need me to get it, right?"

"Yes, girl. Thank you. I've been craving that all day but it's just too damn hot to be walking around. It was so hot in church today I thought I would have to drink the holy water."

"Mom, you are so silly. Where's the dollars?"

"You working. You can't afford some chips and dip—oh, and can you get me some ginger ale too? I have a little bit of an upset stomach."

"Dang, Mom, you gone take all my little tips."

"Come on, Jayd. I spent the last of my little cash filling up my tank. I'll pay you back when I get paid next week."

"OK, Mom. But, don't forget."

Although my mom can work a nerve, I wouldn't mind living like she does when I grow up. She's quite the independent woman. She has her own apartment, her own car, and takes care of herself, no man included. I mean, she dates or whatever, but she doesn't need a man to pay her bills. That's highly unusual for most of the women I know around here.

There are always women fighting over men, whether they're the girlfriends, baby-mamas or whatever. It's just so ghetto, and I'm glad my mother ain't like that. The one time my mother got into an argument with a baby-mama, she said what she had to say in a low, deep tone and then simply walked away from the female, and the dude too. No loud talking, shoe throwing, or hair pulling. It's just not her style. Besides, my mom is pretty fly, and there are always more men. Always. A walk will give me some time to think.

My mom lives on a small street where houses are extremely rare. Apartment buildings have taken their place, but it seems there's at least one family on every block that refuses to sell their home and is still sticking it out.

It's Labor Day weekend, and people are hangin' out all over the place, barbecuing, drinking, smoking, and whatever else they feel like doing. I'm nervous about school starting on Tuesday, especially with this KJ mess still so fresh. It's already nerve-racking just going back to school with new teachers, new clothes, and all. Not to mention the fact that my nemesis, Misty, is on my last nerve. Now this.

"Hey, shorty. I wish I was a pocket on them shorts you wearing," this brotha says as I walk past. He and his homies are hangin' out on the steps of their apartment. I see them every time I come to the store and they always have something to say.

"I just want to be one of them flip-flops on her feet, a sleeve on her shirt, something. Can a brotha holla or what?"

Usually I wouldn't respond and they're used to me doing just that. But today I was fired up and needed to take it out on someone, and this dude will have to do.

I stop and turn on them. "When I walk by here, do I ever speak to y'all?" I ask, shocking the hell out of all of them.

"Well, do I?" I repeat again because they obviously didn't hear me or maybe they just don't know what to say.

"Never mind. The answer is and will always be 'hell no.' So, stop asking."

As I cross the street, leaving them dudes dumbfounded, I walk up the five steps that lead to "The Right Stop" liquor store, thinking about my list of munchies and my impending school drama, when I hear this loud noise from my left. It sounds like a big engine gunning. I turn around and this gray Regal pulls up from out of nowhere it seems. Two dudes in all black jump out and blast the same dude who just tried to holla at me.

"Jayd!" screams Mrs. Ngyuen, the store owner. She grabs my arm, pulls me inside the door, and turns the two huge steel locks.

The gunfire is loud. I'm barely aware of all the screaming inside and outside Mrs. Ngyuen's store.

When the gunfire stops, we hear tires screeching off and nothing else. Something overcomes me.

"Mrs. Ngyuen, open the door. I got to go see if that brotha is OK."

"Jayd, are you crazy? Your mother would have my butt in sling if I let you out. Stay down until police get here," she says in slightly broken English. She and her husband have owned this store for five years now and have seen their fair share of violence, so she knows what to do, but still I persist.

"Now you know that's going to take forever. This is Inglewood, South Central L.A. They ain't gone come soon enough. Let me out, now!" I yell. Finally, she's convinced, but Mrs. Ngyuen ain't moving fast enough for me, so I grab the keys from her hand and open the door myself, before running down the stairs and across the street. He's lying in a pool of blood, eyes wide open, gasping in between bloody breaths of air that just aren't there for him to catch.

As crowded and noisy as it was outside five minutes ago is how empty and quiet it is right now. No one is outside. I see curtains moving in windows so I know folks are watching.

"Somebody, quick. Get me a blanket and some towels. I have to try and stop the bleeding. Hurry, please!" I say frantically to anyone listening. Unfortunately, this isn't the first time I've had to act alone in a crisis situation. Not thinking, I take off my shirt and try to stop the bleeding coming from his chest, arms, and mouth like I learned in health class.

Once the ambulance, police, and other bystanders make their way to the scene to take over, I slowly walk back to my mom's house in a daze. It's been a while since I saw somebody get shot.

I reach my mom's door and put the key in the lock.

"Did you remember the ginger ale?" my mom asks from the kitchen.

"No, Mom. I forgot to get that and everything else too," I say with my bloody tank top in my hands. No matter how many times I see someone get shot or stabbed, I never get used to seeing the blood.

My mom comes out of the kitchen looking like she's about to pounce on me before she takes a loud gasp.

"Jayd! What happened? Are you OK?"

"I'm fine, Mom. Nothing I ain't seen before," I say. I'm tired from work, from KJ, from the shooting, from everything, and I still have to pack up my trash bags–turned–luggage to go home tomorrow.

"Whose blood is this? Are you hurt?" My mom grabs me and takes me into the bathroom.

I want to tell her about everything: the shooting, KJ dumping me, Misty selling me out, everything. But I just can't seem to find the words.

"Mom, I got it. I just want to take a shower and go to bed."

My mother looks like she doesn't know what to do, so she sticks with what she knows.

"Not until you tell Mama what happened. You know how she is. If you don't talk to her tonight and she finds out about it tomorrow, she'll never forgive you." My mom knows like I do that Mama will always have the answer.

After my shower, I notice a pimple brewing on my nose. The drama just never stops. I call Mama and break down everything that happened today.

"Have you been studying your earth lessons, child? You know you have a writing assignment due to me tomorrow, as well as a lab. Have you even started?" Mama asks, almost cooing.

Mama and her damned lessons. As if I don't have enough schoolwork, she makes me memorize formulas for different tinctures and potions. She also makes me write down my dreams and these sayings she calls "affirmations." According to Mama, writing down your wants and desires, or your affirmations, is the same thing as making them come true.

"Mama, after all that happened to me today, that's what you're worried about? My lessons?" I ask, almost offended.

"Jayd, life never slows down for us. It just changes. And you need your lessons to help you deal with the changes. Like that pimple. Don't you have a potion in your notes for that?"

I haven't looked at my notes from Mama's lessons all summer. Before I can answer her, she says, "Study the potion, Jayd, and we'll work on it tomorrow when you get home."

~ 2 ~
Home

*"Woke up quick, at about noon
Just felt that I had to be in Compton soon."*

—EAZY-E

It's midafternoon and everybody's hangin' out for the holiday. When my mom and I pull up to Mama's house, I'm
more than glad; my mom's little '94 Mazda Protégé has a broken air conditioner and a radio I have to hold on my lap.

I get out of the car and start to walk through the backyard
and into the kitchen, but Mama calls me and my mom into
the yard. While walking through the gate, I can hear our
neighbor, Esmeralda, mumbling something under her breath
in Portugese.

Daddy's at the grill barbecuing every part of a pig that can
be cooked, along with some beef ribs, chicken legs, and hot
dogs.

"Hey there, Tweet. How's my favorite granddaughter?"
Daddy asks, giving me a big hug.

"I'm fine, Daddy. Got any tofu on that plate?"

"You know, if it don't bark, squeal, or holla, it ain't allowed
on Daddy's grill."

"Wasn't nobody talking to you, Bryan," Daddy says, giving
Bryan an evil look.

"I thought you was going in the house to get the Dominoes and cards so we can get a game of Spades going on out
here."

"Daddy, you don't want none of this," Bryan says, hitting his chest like he's Shaft.

"Bryan, I can beat you in Spades without a partner, and Daddy taught me how to play," I say, hoping they'll get the hint and let me play. I love playing Dominoes and Spades, especially if there's money at stake.

"Tweet, go on back there with Mama and stay out of men's affairs," Daddy says to me. "Bryan, go get your brothers and tell them to get out here."

A little defeated, I walk back to the small garden area away from the men and notice that the Christmas lights Daddy keeps promising to take down are still on the roof. He did paint the house over the weekend though, a nice dark blue with light gray trim.

"Lil Lynn and Jayd, my two girls. I thought y'all would never get here." Mama's in one of her infamous housedresses that look more like evening wear. Unlike the rest of the neighborhood, Mama's not cooking or partying. Instead, she's in the back making potions and charm bags for her clients.

"I think you and the plumber are the only two people working on Labor Day," my mom says while giving Mama a kiss on the cheek.

Mama bends over, picking up a thick stainless-steel pot filled with some concoction, and passes a spoonful to me to taste.

"It's a lesson, Jayd. You should be able to decipher from the texture, taste, and smell what ingredients are in a potion. What can you tell me about this one?"

"Well, it's green, thick, and gooey, and it smells minty."

"So, what ingredients make up all those things and can be used to kill a pimple?"

"Well, let me think. Gooey must be from the aloe vera plant."

"Very good. And you know aloe can be used to dry out all kinds of blemishes. What else?"

"Okay. The minty smell comes from eucalyptus oil, maybe?"

"Are you asking or telling me? Be sure in your answer, Jayd. Even if you think it's wrong, take a leap of faith that maybe you're right."

"Am I?" I ask, hopeful that my half-assed studying is actually paying off.

"No, you're not. It's tea tree oil. That's why you need to study more and stop worrying about them boys. What's the last ingredient?"

Now she's reminding me of yesterday's pain. My mind is right back to KJ and as far away from this lesson as possible.

"I don't know. Something to make it green?" I say, knowing Mama's getting annoyed with me.

"Jayd, get away from me with that silliness," she says, turning away from me and back to the potion. "One day I'm not going to be here and you're going to wish you were a better student. Your mama was the same way when she was your age," Mama says in a voice meant for my mom. "Out of all of my children, Lynn was the most difficult when it came to learning about her root history. Don't be like your mama, Jayd."

My mom's standing at the gate, hears her, rolls her eyes, and decides it's time for her to go. "It's always fun, but I gotta roll. I'll see you Friday night, baby," my mom says, giving me a kiss on the cheek.

"If you need to talk, you know where to find me." My mom can never stay here too long. I wonder why she thinks I don't mind living here if she can't even visit for more than a few minutes herself.

"She wouldn't have to find you if you would stay your ass put somewhere."

"I love you too, Mama," my mom yells on her way out the yard and to her car.

I sometimes forget that Mama raised my mom too. Mama almost feels like she's my real mother. And my mom feels more like my big sister. It isn't unusual, especially in our neighborhood, but it's still a strange feeling to have two mothers.

Out of the two, Mama is definitely more well rounded. I look at my mom drive away in her little car and then I look at Mama. I can only find one word to describe her: fierce. The sistah is as bad as they come. From head to toe, Mama represents ghetto bougie fab sophistication.

Her favorite place to shop is Nordstrom's. Well, that was before they brought Bloomingdale's to Cali a few years back. Mama's favorite designer is Jones New York, although she also loves Liz Claiborne for her casual wear.

At five foot seven inches with heels—which she's rarely seen without—Mama's not physically a big woman, but she has a large presence. Mama dresses up for everything, especially to go shopping.

Her favorite perfume is Yves St. Laurent's Amarige. She bathes in the stuff, lotions down, and sprays it up. You can get a whiff of her from more than a mile away. Mama stands out around here and she's hated and feared because she's unique.

Mama pretty much ignores Daddy—except when he attacks her "work." I don't understand why they're still together. They haven't slept in the same room since I was a little girl. She doesn't cook for him anymore, nor does she sweat him about all his side women, or "church hussies" as Mama calls them. That's why she stopped going to church. The women talked way too much.

"Lynn Mae is always hanging out with that Mexican lady."

Mama would tell them, *"Esmeralda's from Brazil, not Mexico."*

"Her and that lady be up to no good, I tell you what. They be in that back house conjuring up the devil's work."

Mama would say to those same church women, *"It wasn't the devil's work when you needed a him-never-leave-me-potion for that trifling-ass husband of yours, now was it?"*

"Lynn Mae think she so much better than everybody 'cause she light-skinned with that long, brown wavy hair and them green eyes. I bet they ain't even hers. My sister got a pair just like them at the mall." Then the laughter.

Mama cut her hair short just to shut them up. But even when Mama cut all her hair off, she was still fierce. She got it cut in a real short style, but hella feminine. To me she looks even more beautiful with her hair short. But she couldn't do anything about her eyes.

"Jayd, help me take these things into the house. It's getting late and you have a big day tomorrow."

I pick up the heavy pots, white towels, and other items she uses for her work.

"Did you mix that potion for your pimple like I told you to? I sent you to your mama's with everything you needed so you have no excuse, Jayd. And, what about the No More Drama charm bag I asked you to make last night?"

Damn. I forgot all about my lesson last night. I hope she doesn't make me do it tonight. All I want to do is eat some of my cousin Jay's potato salad and get ready for bed. I still have yesterday on my mind and I didn't sleep well at all last night.

"I'm sorry, Mama. I forgot to read my notes."

Mama reaches into her pocket and hands me a small vial of the potion she was just mixing.

"Take a cotton ball and dab some of that on your pimple. It will be gone by morning," she says, winking at me.

Knowing Mama, the potion for my pimple will not only

work but it'll also make my skin glow or something a little extra like that. I'm glad because I can't have none of them boys seeing me with a big pimple on my nose on the first day of school.

After I help Mama bring the rest of the stuff into the house, I eat a big bowl of potato salad and get ready for tomorrow, the first day back at Drama High. I would call my girls to see if there's any last minute info I need before the first day, but I want to take advantage of the fact that all the men are outside, leaving the bathroom free and clear for a nice, hot bath without anyone banging on the door.

After my bath, I make my bed. I haven't slept in it for a couple of weeks because I've been over at my mom's since summer school ended, and I know Mama didn't change the sheets for me. Domestic work just ain't her thing. As I turn down my sheets to get ready for bed, I feel the potion working already. I wish she could make me a potion to change the past. I still can't understand why KJ doesn't want me anymore. Is sex really that important?

So much to think about. I hope we got some new brothas this year, 'cause the old ones are tired. I wonder what my girls are wearing, and the boys too. I also think about seeing KJ in the morning. Maybe it won't be so bad.

Before closing my eyes I pray I can get into the bathroom in the morning without sitting on a wet toilet seat or smelling someone's funky butt. I hate sharing a bathroom with all these dudes.

Last year I asked my mom if I could live with her. At least it would be just us girls. But, according to my mom, she's still in the prime of her life. She dates, hangs out with her girlfriends, and goes to the gym every night after work, which means she can't be saddled with a teenager.

"I just don't have the time to be running after you, Jayd. Besides, what would Mama say if I took you away from her?

And brought you here, to South Central? Mama would have a fit and I would never hear the end of it. Stay where you are. Mama and Daddy can take better care of you than I can."

And that was the end of that. There's no convincing my mom of anything once she has her mind made up. She doesn't have that normal mother guilt Mama has. If I beg hard enough I can usually get my way with Mama. But not with my mom. She's rock hard when it comes to my pleading, especially if whatever I'm pleading for involves any effort on her part. It hurts sometimes.

Finally, before falling asleep, I pray for a mellow first day of school.

~ 3 ~
From Hood to Hood

*"It's time to take a trip to the suburb
Let them see a nigga invasion."*

—ICE CUBE

5:30 A.M.

"**B**liiiing!!!!"

Dang, I hate that sound. If the Tasmanian devil's little face wasn't so cute, I think I would fling this alarm clock across the room. With my luck, it would hit Mama in the head or something. I haven't had to hear it this early all summer long. It's September again and the alarm clock's loud-ass ring will again be my morning companion.

"Jayd, go on and get up now. You don't want to be late for your first day of school."

"All right, Mama. I'm up."

As I crawl out of my stuffy twin size bed, identical to my grandmother's, I second guess what I've decided to wear. My outfit is hanging on the back of the bedroom door with all of Mama's clothes that need to go to the cleaner's or be hung in the closet.

I picked out my outfit a week ago when I went shopping at the South Bay Galleria; Express was having a sale. Now, you know a sistah couldn't pass that up. Being a little on the thick side, I don't have a lot of options for clothing that will fit me good, but Express always has my size.

My outfit is tight. I got some low-waist, boot-cut jeans, a little baby-doll type shirt in lavender like the ones Free used to wear on 106th and Park, and some boots from Baker's. You know I'm looking too fine for the first day.

As I make it to the door to get my clothes off the hanger, I remember I let Nellie borrow my sweater. It's the only thing I have to match my outfit. I'll have to try and catch Nellie before she leaves the house and ask her to bring it to school.

I can't be caught in the South Bay without a sweater, as cold and foggy as it is by the beach. I used to not worry about it, just let my hair fro out until the afternoon sun melted the fog away. But after me and KJ hooked up, I began to care a little more.

"Jayd, make sure you don't take too long in the bathroom. Bryan got a new job and he don't need no reason not to go."

"All right, Mama. I'll hurry up."

That's the thing about living in a house with seven other people—there's never much time in the bathroom. I also hate not having any space to myself. Not only do I have to share a room with my grandmother, but I also have no closet space, dresser drawers, or privacy. Every sixteen-year-old needs her privacy, ya feel me?

Mama and my grandfather need to go back to sharing a room and all the boys should sleep in the den. That way I can have my own room, since I'm the only girl. Mama says I'm only thinking of myself and that the boys should be with the boys and the girls with the girls. Call me selfish, but I still like my idea better.

As it stands now, Mama and I are in one room at the end of our very small hallway. The bathroom is at the other end next to the room Daddy, Bryan, and Jay share. My other three uncles, Carl, Sean, and Junior, all sleep in the den.

The house sounds big, but it ain't. It's actually very small and not big enough for all these folks up in here. I have to be careful as I stumble my way toward the bathroom. Bryan must've just turned the floor heater on to knock off the morning chill and it wouldn't be the first time I burn myself.

I open the door to Daddy and the boy's room before going into the bathroom. I try not to wake anybody up. Bryan, though, is already up and in his van, smoking a joint or doing something else he thinks is revolutionary.

Without any dresser or closet space of my own, I have to keep all of my stuff in my two big black Hefty garbage bags on the left side of the closet. I don't have much, but what I do have I like to keep as neat and as orderly as possible. One bag has all my underwear, T-shirts, tank tops, and head rags in it. It also has all my toiletries, my towels, and anything else I might need to access quickly in the dark. The other bag has the rest of my clothes and my other two pairs of shoes.

I usually pick out my clothes before the boys get home in the evening. That way I can consider my outfits in peace and lay it out on Daddy's bed or on Bryan's bottom bunk to make sure everything matches. We don't have a floor-length mirror, so I usually stand on top of Mama's bed and look at my outfit in her vanity mirror once she gets up, if it's not too late in the morning.

So, here I am, digging through my trash bags—now turned dresser drawers—looking for a clean towel and the rest of my bath stuff. In this house, if you don't keep all your things stashed away, they'll either end up used, abused, or in the pawn shop on Central and Rosecrans.

"Dang, Jayd. You straight look like a girl Lil' Bow Wow with them cornrows and that thug rag on your head," Bryan says, coming in the bedroom smelling like weed.

"Shut up, Bryan, and move outta my way. I get first crack at the bathroom. I got to catch the 6:35 A.M. bus, so step back," I say, pushing him out of the way. My uncle Bryan is nine years older than me, but he still acts my age.

"Why you always got to be so pushy? That's why you ain't got no man." And with that last stab at my ego, he goes into the kitchen to eat a couple bowls of corn flakes. Though Bryan can work a nerve sometimes, secretly, he's my favorite uncle.

Bryan is the only one in the family to go to any type of college and is now a DJ for the independent radio station KPFK. It's real cool having an uncle who's a DJ. I get hip to all kinds of music I would normally never hear, like all the stuff he grew up listening to: Run DMC, Public Enemy, Salt 'n' Pepa, KRS 1, and Sade just to name a few. But, he also plays hellafied oldies too, like Tina Turner, The OJays, Bob Marley, Marvin Gaye, and so on. Mama says Bryan has a gifted ear and mind, and that I have a gifted soul to be able to appreciate all that good music.

And appreciate it I do. The music out nowadays don't even compare to what my uncle plays on his show. He calls it *The Other Side of Compton* in dedication to the history of our fine city. You see, I didn't know this, but back in the day, Central Boulevard—which we live near—used to be the happening spot for jazz. Yes, jazz. Not gangsta rap or drive-bys, but jazz music.

Now, don't get me wrong—we still love NWA and Easy E, Dr. Dre, Snoop, and all them—but it's nice to know our musical roots go deeper, ya feel me?

"Jayd, most of them g's in the street don't know half the stuff I'm talking about. That's why I do my show."

"But you ain't makin' no money, Bryan. And Mama says if you ain't makin' no money, you gonna have to pay her and Daddy back for school."

"Jayd, life is about more than money."

"Yeah, well, tell that to Mama when she writing checks for your student loans."

"Yeah, yeah. That's why I got the job at Miracle Market to help Mama out. But Jayd, you gotta listen to this right here."

When Bryan gets passionate about something, he really feels it and wants everyone else to feel it as well.

Everyone is real proud of Bryan. He got into IT&T and went for it. He always knew he wanted to be a music engineer/producer. He went to school for two years and just graduated in June.

He plays stuff like Portishead and Pink, Kina and Lenny Kravitz. In grade school they made fun of him for being "different." He was the kid with the "X" shirt and the afro with a pick in his head. He was a teenager in the nineties—you know, Jodeci, Jordan, and Jeri Curls named Wave Neuveau. But there was nothing revolutionary about Bryan's homies.

Most of Bryan's friends from around the block are either in jail, dead, or doing something to end up in jail or dead. Bryan's had his share of minor run-ins with the law, but now he's just trying to do right.

That's why he got a job at the radio station—so he could exercise his political voice through music. Each night he has a theme. One night he might be feeling real spiritual and he'll play some India Airie or Jill Scott. Another night he might be feeling revolutionary and play KRS 1 or Bob Marley. Sometimes he might feel soulful and drop some Nina Simone and Dextor Gordon on his listeners.

His absolute favorite artist is Sade. He swears he's going to go to Jamaica and win her away from her baby daddy.

"Watch, Jayd. I'm gonna be a big-time DJ and I'm gonna be in Jamaica covering the annual island festival and she's gonna be one of the artists."

"When have you ever heard of Sade performing at one of them festivals? They're usually dancehall and rap artists, Bryan."

"The year I'm supposed to meet my wife will be the year

she's there. Now, as I was saying, she's gonna be coming up off stage after performing, glistening with sweat. And she'll see me behind stage. Our eyes will meet. I'll tell her she's the most beautiful woman God ever created. And she'll say she's dreamed of meeting me and I'll say . . ."

"Oh, Sade, forgive me! I usually keep my stalker identity on the low, but I just can't help it!"

"Whatever, Jayd. It ain't worse than you dreaming about that Black dude on CSI."

"Oh no, I will marry Gary Dourdan and we will have beautiful babies together. I'm already knowing."

"Jayd, that dude is old enough to be your daddy."

"And Sade is old enough to be your mama."

"But I'm grown. So, that's okay. You, on the other hand, are still wet behind the ears, know what I'm sayin'?"

Bryan's such a know-it-all. He always gets the last word.

"Jayd. Jayd! Get out the bathroom or you gone miss your bus," Mama says from the hallway. I finish getting dressed, take one last look in the mirror, noticing Mama's pimple potion's worked overnight and grab all my stuff to put back in the closet.

I hate having to get up so early to go to school. Redondo Beach is just too far to go every morning, I swear. It wasn't so bad when KJ was taking me to school over the summer. But now that we've split, I'm back to taking the bus.

I don't know what I'd do without the Metro bus. My mom says when she was growing up it was called the RTD and everybody who rode it would call it the "rough, tough, and dirty" bus. I have to say it ain't that bad now. It's still not clean like the Torrance or Gardena buses I transfer to when I go to school, but they could be a lot worse.

I usually get to school about 7:45 A.M., ten minutes before

the warning bell rings. This gives me just enough time to get to my locker, catch my girls before class, and get the necessary info for the day like which couples broke up, who got caught doing what, any dirt on the faculty. You know, important stuff that keeps me in the loop.

6:30 A.M.

The first time I took the bus from Compton to the South Bay was the longest damn bus ride ever. It was September and scorching hot, just like this morning.

As I walk down the block toward Alondra to catch my first bus, I'm already sweating from the morning sun. Mr. Gatlin is outside trimming his already immaculate lawn. Every year he gives his house a fresh coat of sparkly green paint with silver trim to match the Buick in his driveway. He used to be a marine, so he always wears his uniform. I've never seen him wear anything else.

I don't speak to Mr. Gatlin. He's the only neighbor who scares me. I'll never forget when I was about six or seven years old and he called the police on me because I accidentally walked on his grass. Well, it was an accident the first time. The second and third time was just to make him mad. Luckily though, he lives on the other side of the street, and I can avoid passing directly by him.

I have to catch the 6:35 bus to connect to the 7:15 in Gardena, which will get me to South Bay High at 7:45. Here we go again. Another bus ride. Another year of high school at South Bay High. Cute clothes, hatin' girls. Cute boys, more hatin' girls. But my cornrows are in full effect, no matter what Bryan says. He really can't talk, still rocking the Jeri Curl, even though I don't think they sell the juice for it anymore.

I reach for my cell phone, barely remembering to text

message Nellie about bringing my sweater to school with her. Since her mom takes her to school, she doesn't have to take the bus.

7:45 A.M.

By the time I get to Redondo Beach, it's foggy and about 10 degrees cooler than it is in Compton. It's amazing how in the various parts of Los Angeles County the weather can be so drastically different. That's why I usually carry a sweater and scarf in my bag.

As soon as I exit the bus, the fresh salty smell of the ocean hits me in a breeze. The bus lets me off at the top of a hill, which is directly across from the main part of the campus. There's no crosswalk between the bus stop and the campus, so I'm forced to take the long way around.

It's a good ten-minute walk down the hill and back up again. I do this everyday, twice a day. It keeps my legs in shape. The walk also gives me a little time to daydream about living in houses like the ones lining the street across from my school.

This neighborhood is filled with big, beautiful modern homes with small yards. The houses vary in color, but all look pretty much the same: two stories, three-car garages, and immaculately manicured lawns with roses or some other kind of fancy flowers lining the property. The whole neighborhood looks like the projects for rich folks. All the houses on my block except for one are single-story homes. The Andersons started building a second story onto their house years ago, but never quite finished.

The cars parked in the driveways in the South Bay are either Range Rovers, Volvos, or Mercedes Benzs. The kids that live here are balling out of control and don't even know it. Most of the cars also have ski racks and boat hooks on the back. These are the folks who have weekday cars and week-end cars.

As I look at these homes, I wonder about how the families living in them operate. I'm sure they all have their fair share of skeletons. It may be a different neighborhood, but the same kind of drama happens everywhere. Well, maybe not exactly the same.

I see some of my schoolmates' parents outside leaving for work. These White folks hate seeing my Black self walk up the street. They probably think I'm gone steal one of their lawn ornaments or key their car or something. Sometimes I'll slow down and stare at the White people coming out of their houses in the morning to put some fear in these snooty people. I know it's wrong, but so is stereotyping. I don't need any extra drama this morning, so I just keep walking down the hill to South Bay High.

~ 4 ~
The First Day Back

"No more drama in your life"

—MARY J. BLIGE

It's my junior year and things will be different. "No more drama." Ain't that what Mary said? That's what I'm going for, a smooth, drama-free year, unlike last year, my first year at Drama High, and believe me, after last year, this school has earned its nickname.

As I enter the school I think I don't want to see Misty this morning. She's certainly a large reason this school has so much drama. I had enough of that girl over the summer. It's weird she wasn't on the bus this morning. Maybe she'll miss today altogether. That would make today an ideal first day, along with not seeing KJ's punk ass.

This morning just before I left, Mama prayed I would have a peaceful year. She also gave me a special tiny bag filled with crystals and other good-luck charms. It's supposed to go in my purse, but I got one of them little fake Coach bags from the Swap Meet, so it wasn't gone fit in there. I had to put it in my backpack instead. So let's see if this "No More Drama" charm bag will work from my backpack. Hopefully this is the beginning of a peaceful day at Drama High.

7:50 A.M.

As I walk down the main hall reading the schedule I had printed out two weeks ago at registration, I notice the walls have been painted a bright, bright white this year and the gray-colored lockers are now blue. It looks hot compared to last year. That's the difference in the schools on the White side of town. Every summer they get all kinds of improvements.

My locker's in the middle of the main hall this year—the most crowded locker space of all. I hate going to the main hall. Before I get to my locker, I realize my schedule is wrong—again. I'm annoyed with myself for not having noticed sooner. When I first came to this school, they did the same thing. They put me on the R.E. track, instead of the A.P. track. I just don't have the patience for this today.

My very first day at South Bay High last year was just as confusing and drama-filled. My mom didn't want me to go to the schools in the area she lived in and my dad, out of spite—even all these years later—because my mom left him, stopped paying for my education. We couldn't afford the private school my father had enrolled me in for sixth through ninth grades, so I couldn't go back there.

I put up a big fight to at least stay in the same area so I could be with my homies, but Mama was not having me going to Compton or Centennial High School. And all the other schools between Compton and the South Bay were full. So, for a while I didn't have anywhere to go to school.

Mama was upset and told my mom to find me somewhere to go to school "come hell or high water," one of Mama's favorite sayings. So my mother found a girlfriend who has an address in Redondo Beach and, like magic, I'm a proud student of South Bay High.

Misty's the very first person I met. She's an office aide. Lucky for Misty, her mother is the secretary for the Attendance Office. Otherwise, with her grades, she would never have been any kind of aide.

*   *   *

"Hello. You look lost. Are you lost? This is the Attendance Office."

"Yeah, I guess so. I'm looking for the Enrollment Office. It's my first day and I need to turn these papers in."

"Yeah, I know where that is. I'll show you. My name is Misty, Misty Truewell. It's my first year here too. Luckily, my mom got a job here, otherwise, I would've gone to a school in my hood and that wouldn't have been cool, know what I'm saying? I talk a lot, I know, but that's just me. So, what's your name, where you from, got a man?"

Already Misty and I were cool because she was straightforward and friendly, like me. She talked with a slight Spanish accent and looked like she could be J. Lo's short, plump cousin. She told me her mom was Puerto Rican and her dad was Black. I could already tell she was mixed.

At 4 feet 9 inches and 170 pounds, Misty was a ball of energy, and because I liked her I decided to answer all her questions—even the last one, which was still quite complicated.

"My name is Jayd. I'm from Compton, and no, I don't have a man, anymore."

"Anymore? Sounds like some boy drama to me, but we'll get to that later," Misty says, looping her arm into mine as we continue walking down the main hall.

"So, you're from Compton. Where in Compton? There are a lot of Black folk here from Compton. Actually, most of the Black folk here are, including myself. So which side you live on? I live right off of Caldwell and Wilmington in Nutty Block. You know where that is?"

I couldn't believe it. This sistah lived right around the corner from me and I had never before set eyes on her. Not at the park, the nail shop, or the liquor store. She must have not come outside much. Mama says there are no coincidences in life, and I think she's right. Misty and I were destined to meet.

"Yeah, I do know where that is. It's my hood too. I live on Gunlock, where do you live?"

"Really? I live on Kemp. We're right around the corner from each other. Isn't that great? We can be best friends. We can come to school together—you take the bus? We can walk each other home—you know how to do hair? What about braids? Oooh, girl, this is gonna be so tight. Oooh, what classes you takin'? We should take all of the same classes so we can do our homework together too. We can be like sisters."

Cousins from hell is more like what we became.

As I approach the Main Office, I notice that it got a fresh coat of white paint as well.

"Good morning and welcome back to South Bay High. What can I help you with?" Mrs. Cole, the school secretary, says.

"I was given the wrong schedule and need to know where to go this morning."

"I can help you with that," she says, taking my schedule. "This shouldn't take too long. Why don't you go ahead and have a seat while I make sure all your papers are in order, and then you will go to the Counseling Office and see Mr. Adelezi. He'll help you pick out your classes and put you on the right track."

"Thank you, Mrs. Cole."

At least this year I don't have Misty trailing behind me asking me a bunch of questions. Her nosey butt is probably just waiting to annoy another new girl this year.

There are five counselors, one for each grade and one for "special circumstances," whatever that means. Mr. Adelezi is the eleventh grade counselor. His office is a small, cramped space with only enough room for his desk and two tall file cabinets. I sit in the only available chair for guests.

"Good morning, Mr. Adelezi. My name is Jayd and I need to change my classes," I say as he looks at me through thin-framed, out-of-style glasses. He's smiling like something's funny.

"Well, Jayd, let's take a look at your paperwork." Mr. Adelezi seems pretty cool, for a counselor.

"I would like to continue on the A.P. track," I say, handing my schedule across his desk.

Mama told me to be firm when choosing my classes because sometimes people don't have my best interest at heart. When we registered at Family Christian, my old school, they almost refused me entry into honors classes. They only let me have my classes after Mama came up there and took care of business. Not at South Bay though; it's too far. So when problems arise, I have to handle them myself.

"All right, Miss Jayd, here's your schedule. Now all you need to do is pick a P.E. elective."

Now this is new. A P.E. elective? What other electives are there in P.E. other than physical education?

"I don't understand—a P.E. elective?"

"Yes. Now that you're in the eleventh grade you can pick from a wide range of activities to participate in for your physical education requirement—if you're on the advanced placement track. There's general P.E., swimming, surfing—where you actually walk to the beach . . ."

"I can leave campus for class?"

"Yes, Jayd. Now, as I was saying, there's surfing, synchronized swimming, track, cheerleading, flag, spirit squad, football—but that's for boys only—soccer, softball, baseball—but, that's also for boys only—gymnastics, and dance class. That's about it."

I can't believe this—a choice of P.E. classes. This school does have some perks after all. If my hair wasn't pressed, I might take up that surfing class just so I could walk to the beach everyday. Coming from Compton, the beach is like a field-trip destination, but I love the ocean. I have a natural—shall we say—respect for the ocean. It's so powerful and unpredictable. But, nah, a sistah can't be getting her hair wet everyday. Mama would kill me. So, dance class was of course the natural choice.

"I'll take dance class."

Mr. Adelezi prints out my schedule.

"OK, Jayd. Just take this temporary schedule. Make sure each teacher signs your schedule and that you get it back to me at the end of the day so I can put your classes into the main system and print you a permanent schedule. You can pick it up in the morning."

"Thanks, Mr. Adelezi."

As I walk back toward my locker I see the cliques already starting to claim their territory. This year I hope to avoid them all, especially South Central, the Black clique. I know KJ and Misty are already hangin' with the crew, inspecting all the new students.

A lot of mess—dramatic type stuff—always happens whenever I venture to South Central. I swear you hear all these bad stories about Compton and just as many about South Central. All the Compton and South Central stories aren't true, but Ice Cube had it dead on in *Boyz from the Hood*. South Central ain't the place to be caught after dark.

All my life I've lived in Compton and nothing violent or crazy has ever happened to me—outside of my own family drama, that is. But, the minute I step foot into South Central, there is some drama going on like the drive-by down the street from my mom's house last weekend. So, why would I want to hang out there voluntarily, be it the real South Central or the clique? And why would they name it that, anyway? Even when Black folks have a clique it has to be ghetto. My people, my people, I tell you.

~ 5 ~
The Cliques

*"You must be honest and true to the next
Don't be phony and expect one not to flex."*

—A TRIBE CALLED QUEST

I quickly learned about the cliques here at South Bay High my first year. Misty, of course, was my personal tour guide, giving me the 411 on South Bay, including which cliques were cool and which were to be avoided. She also showed me where the bathrooms were, introduced me to the cool teachers and administrators, as well as pointed out the most popular and least desirable people. You know, the usual new student info.

During my first year at Drama High, learning about the cliques was my first real education, as it's always important to know who is who and where they "belong." Not much has changed in the year I've been here, at least as far as the cliques are concerned.

As I reach my locker and fumble with the combination lock, I see the cliques gathering to recruit new members. There are too many to count, but five main cliques run this campus. You have the athletes and cheerleaders, the Drama Club Clique, which is the one I belong to, the Associated Student Body and followers' clique, the Latino clique—which they call the Barrio—and then there's South Central, which is made up of the thirty-five or so Black people attending this school. The Barrio and South Central cliques hang right next to each other in the main lunch courtyard.

The athletes and cheerleaders are of course the most popular kids around and get the most perks like getting to leave campus early at least once a week for sporting events. They also hold the most events on campus, and because they control the main schedule, they're the most powerful clique. For example, if the Drama Club clique wants to host a picnic or something, they have to go to the student activities coordinator, who just happens to be a cheerleader, and ask for an available date. More than likely, all the good dates are already reserved for the athletes and cheerleaders events, and the Drama Club will just have to settle for whatever date the cheerleader/student activities coordinator gives them.

But, the Drama Club has their own kind of power. Last year, I guess they got tired of being teased for their dark goth look and put on a spoof during lunch of the athletes and cheerleaders. It's the funniest thing I've ever seen at this school and that's why I joined the club. We had the girls with pink hair and eyebrow rings in cheerleader outfits imitating all the popular girls. And the drama guys, whose voices are still a little too high for high school, wore football uniforms, pretending to be the cool jocks. Oh my God, I laughed so hard. The Drama Club wore their costumes for the rest of the day, just to rub it in.

To say the least, the athletes and cheerleaders didn't like this little stunt at all. They didn't laugh not once. They're just too uptight and popular for their own good. Well, they got even with the Drama Club by canceling their programs for the rest of the year, due to "scheduling conflicts." Whatever. They just have too much power to be students. In my opinion no clique should have any real power over any other clique. That kind of power gets dangerous.

Speaking of danger, as I near my locker, I hear a familiar Spanish accent calling my name. I turn to see my girl Marguerita Lorena Santa Cristina Franco—or Maggie as she goes by in class because the teachers butcher her name. "What's up, chica? How was your summer?" Marguerita says. Maggie hangs with El Barrio. This group is not to be played with. They're hella cool, once you get to know them. They're probably the largest clique of them all. That's because they don't discriminate, as long as you can speak Spanish—or at least make an effort to learn, like I do—then you're in.

"Marguerita, girl, *¿qué pasa?* My summer was cool, working and whatnot. How about you?"

"Girl, we just kicked it all summer in Mexico *con mis abuelita y mis tías.*"

"That's cool, chica. *¿Dónde es tu novio, Juan?*" I ask, wondering where her other half is. Juan and Marguerita are one of the most popular couples in school.

"Here comes my man now," Maggie says, looking past me. Juan is just a few steps away. He nods in my direction while putting his arm around Maggie. I can't help but smile at them. They're such a cute couple.

Speak of the devil; here he comes strolling up the hall with his crew right behind him.

"*¡Hasta luego!* Jayd. I'm going to let Juan have the pleasure of walking me to class."

"See you later, Marguerita."

The Barrio clique is hella tight. They believe in "one for all." If you step to them disrespecting, you know you better watch your back because they don't play.

Like last year, this White boy rolled up shouting all kinds of racist BS at them and South Central. The White boy, Chris, was a skinhead—they have a clique too, if you can call it that—and decided it was White Power Day at South Bay High. So, he walked up to Marguerita's man Juan, the leader of El Barrio, and told him to go back to Mexico and called him a "*mojado*," or wetback. Not good at all. Juan told Chris he wasn't from Mexico, but Costa Rica, and that Chris better step out of his territory before he gets hurt.

Next thing we knew, Chris pulled out a knife and said, "To hell with all the Blacks and Mexicans ruining the White South Bay High," and tried to shank Juan. Juan beat Chris's ass so bad, they had to take that boy to the emergency room. Yeah, you don't mess with the brothers and sisters from the Barrio.

The only clique that really doesn't get into too much mess is the Associated Student Body, or ASB, clique. They try to unite everyone. They truly have the school's best interest at heart, or so they say. The president, Reid Connelly, is a little George W. Bush in training.

The ASB clique does have the most clout with the principal and other administrators in the school, however. They're always going to conferences representing the school here and there. It's like they're our public relations clique, keeping the South Bay High name intact. And here's the president now, to pitch his promises for the year, I assume.

"Hey, Jayd. Are you interested in renewing your membership with the ASB this year?"

"Reid, can I get my locker open before you start handing out pamphlets?"

"Oh, sure, Jayd. My bad. Let me help you with that."

Reid's an okay guy. He's also a member of ROTC and is dressed in uniform today. He's not a bad-looking dude, just not my type. He's a little too anal for my taste. It's one thing to date a White boy, a whole other thing to date one whose family is in the military. They tend to be a little too patriotic for me.

"There you go. The locks are a little sticky because of the new paint, so you have to pull it hard until it loosens up."

"Thanks, Reid."

"No, thank *you*. And, I hope to see you at the ASB meetings this year. First one's next week."

"You never give up, do you?" I say, half-flirting. It's good to
keep it light and friendly with powerful people.

"Never, Jayd. Surrendering is for the weak, unless you sur-
render to ASB."

"Go harass someone else, Reid," I say, laughing. "And,
thanks again for getting my locker open."

"No problem."

I've been a member of most of the cliques at one time or
another, and continue to be an honorary member of most.
Even though my Spanish is sketchy, they still let me hang in
the Barrio when I feel like it. I can't help it if I cross over,
though I don't really like the idea of cliques to begin with. I
remember when Misty first introduced me into South
Central. It was just like I thought it would be.

*"Hey, everybody. I want y'all to meet the newest member
of our ghetto fabulous family. This is Jayd. Jayd, this is
everybody."*

*"Hey, girl, what's up? I'm LaShae, but everybody around
here calls me Shae. This is Dominique, Peppa, Quisha, and
this here is Tony, my man. So make sure I don't hear nothing
about you not knowing who he is because I will beat any
girl down for my Tony."*

*"Yeah, like anybody wants your man anyway, Shae. But,
thanks for the friendly intros," says Quisha.*

*"Dang, Tony, you need to control your girl. She act like
you can't speak for yourself," says this tall, fine, brown-
skinned, gorgeous piece of something sweet.* I thought I
would pass out right there, but I managed to stay on my feet
long enough to meet KJ for the first time.

"What's crackin', Jayd? I'm KJ. This here is my homey

C Money, and my other homey Del. Welcome to South Bay High. Hope to see you at the basketball games. You know we're the stars of the team, right? Well, I'm sure Oprah herself will fill you in," he says, with a smile pointing at Misty.

"Who you callin' Oprah?" Misty says, scrunching up her face, pretending to be offended. "That's cool, though. I wouldn't mind getting paid like Oprah, you know what I'm sayin'?"

"Yeah, I feel you on that one," Shae says. "She's the richest Black woman I've ever heard of. She must be the first Black millionaire."

"Well, actually, she isn't," I interject. "The first Black millionaire is this other sister named Madame C. J. Walker. She invented the pressing comb, so you can see why she became a millionaire," I say, trying to make a joke. As soon as I said it, I knew I shouldn't have. Everybody just got kind of quiet and looked at Misty, and then looked at me like "who the hell are you again and where did you come from?"

"Thank you, Encyclopedia Britannica for that lovely and helpful information," Shae says. She sounded pissed, especially because Tony and the other boys were smiling at me, particularly KJ.

"Well, it looks like we got ourselves a brain in South Central. Where did you say you're from, Jayd?" asks Del. He turned out to be the joker of the crew.

"I'm from Compton, Del, and you?"

"Yeah, me too. But you don't sound like you're from Compton. Sistahs I know don't go around quoting Black history and stuff."

"And, what exactly should I sound like?" I hate when people make generalizations about me and where I'm from. This happens all the time, and it always gets me hot.

"You should sound like us and you don't. We don't need

*no goodie goodies hangin' around here. Maybe she belongs
in another clique, Misty. Not over here with us," Shae says.*
And, just like that, I made my first enemy in Shae.

*"Dang, Shae, the girl has been here for all of a minute
and you're already trying to call the drop squad on her like
she's a sell-out or something. All she did was drop some
knowledge on us, and what's wrong with that?" KJ says,
coming to my defense like a knight in shining armor and
fresh Jordans.*

*"Well, she's on the A.P. track, so we won't be seeing her in
any of our classes, if that makes you happy, Shae."*

Why did Misty have to open her big mouth and tell everybody that? Looking back on it now, it was a typical hater
move. But at the time I was just embarrassed and wanted to
roll out. That's the problem with cliques. If you don't fit their
narrow guidelines, you're not one of them. And in this case I
was glad to be an outsider.

*"The A.P. track? Speaking of first, I think you may be the
first non-White person on that track ever. They should give
you a plaque or something," Del says. Everybody laughs, including KJ.*

"Yeah, let's give Miss Smarty a medal or something."
There is Shae again. What was her problem with me? I had
just met the girl and already she was just asking for it. Shae's
little nasty attitude was enough to make the ghetto come out
in me.

*"Uhmm, you know what, Shae? If you have such a prob-
lem with me, there are several ways we can solve it. But personally, I don't see how you can already feel so threatened
by me. Please, don't worry. I don't want to take your spot in
this precious clique or your mute man. On the real, though,
you can save that foul attitude of yours for somebody else,
'cause I don't take too kindly to your mouth. You don't
know me, so be careful what you say to me."*

Shae looks shocked, like she doesn't know what to say, but her eyes never leave me. Everybody gets still. Misty's expression says "oh, no she didn't just go there," and everybody else is just waiting to see what will happen next.

"Well, I guess we do have a Compton girl after all. Welcome to Drama High, Jayd. I think you're gonna do just fine here," KJ says, trying to lighten the mood. Finally, Shae speaks up.

"Yeah, I guess we do," she says. I stand my ground while she tries to think of something to say.

"Jayd, why don't I show you around the rest of the campus before the bell rings? We'll catch up with y'all later." Misty grabs my arm, spins me around, and starts walking real fast across the lunch area, away from South Central.

"Girl, you don't know Shae like that. You shouldn't have said that. Now Shae is going to be all up in your business, trying to hate on you in ways you can't even imagine. She is real protective of her man Tony, even though he is as ugly as sin. But, she's like that with all of the girls, not just you. Why did you say that to her? Damn, now I know there's going to be some drama behind this mess. Shae don't let nothing slide."

"Are you afraid of her or something?" I ask Misty, because she sure did sound like it to me.

"Yes! And you should be too. Shae used to be a member of Piru Street gang and her man Tony still is, even though he don't look like it. They both got kicked out of Centennial for robbing a teacher. How they got here I just don't know, but we try not to mess with them and let them think they run South Central."

"Well, Misty, I really don't give a damn about all that. Nobody runs me, and they and you can have South Central. I'm not into cliques and I don't let nobody punk me, not even some broad from Piru. If she wants to fight me, fine.

Bring it on. But it needs to be known from jump that I may be smart and I may not fit y'all's little image of what a girl from Compton is, but don't nobody talk mess to Jayd Jackson and get away with it."

"I see that and hey, for the record, I agree with you. I'm glad you said something to that hoochie. I think you're the first, maybe the second girl to stand up to her. She goes on like that all the time. This girl named Mickey is the only other person I know who has stood up to her."

"Where is she now? Don't tell me dead or crippled or something."

"No, she's cool. She hangs out with this girl named Nellie. They're too good for us common Black folk, so they just kick it wherever, I guess. I really don't pay much attention to them. But the only reason Mickey got away with that is because her boyfriend is a member of a gang, and Tony didn't want no trouble with him over Shae's mouth."

"Oh, so he can speak when he wants to."

"Yeah, he can, but he don't talk much. He's a man of action, so I hear, not words. He leaves the mess talking to Shae."

"Look, Misty, just like you said I don't know Shae like that, don't nobody up here know me like that."

"Yeah, but you can't just be going around telling people off on your first day here, Jayd. You gotta let people feel you out first and you feel them out. It's better to be thought of as shy and quiet at first, and then come out with that ghetto attitude."

"I thought that's what I did," I say with an edge of sarcasm.

"No, Jayd. You didn't do that at all. Girl, you have to play the game if you're going to survive one day here. This is Drama High, no matter what it says on the front of the school. If you want to walk through here every day without

getting into a fight or having people hate on you all year for no reason, you're going to have to come off that high horse you on and respect the rules of the game."

But I've learned playing games always leads to more drama, which is why Misty is always in some mess. Boys like to play games too, although that's on a whole different level. Unfortunately, we all get dragged into a mess sometimes, especially when we think we're in love.

~ 6 ~
The Drama Begins

"They smile in your face
All the time they want to take your place, them backstabbers."

—THE OJAYS

By the time I get my new schedule and get back to my locker, the hall is packed with students. Everybody's rushing all over, looking for their lockers, saying "Hi" to their friends, rolling their eyes at their enemies. Everybody's looking fly for their first day too, in whatever gear they got on. Even teachers are dressed up for their new students. And, everyone's running late.

As I close my locker door, quietly hoping I can get it open later without any help, I notice Trecee down the hall talking to this girl I don't know and pointing at me. She's in a powder blue sweat suit with a little navy blue tank top underneath, wearing her hair in gold-and-blue box braids to match her outfit, and big gold hoops hang from her ears. That's just Trecee's style: tacky. I'm wondering what she could want with me when she and her friend start walking toward me and I know I'll find out soon enough.

"Didn't you learn not to mess with other people's property?" she says, looking like she's about to punch me. Her friend stands behind Trecee in a way that says she's got her back.

"Who are you talking to?" I ask, hardening my expression

and ready for the fight, though I have no idea whose property she's referring to.

"I'm talking to you and I know all about you and KJ," Trecee says.

I can't believe she's stepping to me over some bullshit with KJ. I mean, first of all, I am already pissed and hurt because of our breakup, so I don't want too much to do with him now anyway. Second of all, he can't want her behind no way, especially not after dealing with a queen like myself. So, what she is trippin' over is really beyond me.

So, anyway, this broad wants to "warn me" that KJ is her man now, and I had better stay away from him. "WHATEVER!" is exactly what I say to her. She ain't got no clout with nobody, especially not with none of the people that I know.

You see, Trecee is one of them unnoticeable kinda girls. She knows just as well as everybody else that she ain't cute, she ain't smart, and sure enough she don't dress tight. But, unlike cute girls like me and my girls, she'll give up the cookies to just about anybody.

I mean, I'm still a virgin and I ain't thinking about giving up the cookies no time soon. Well, I almost did to Kalvinice, or KJ as he likes to be called, and you can see why. I mean, what the hell kind of name is Kalvinice? And then to name somebody that twice, 'cause yes, he's a junior. Anyway, that brotha had me sprung. I was in love with him and he dogged me good, real good.

KJ's the most popular Black cat at school. He's on the basketball team, and he's pretty good. He's cute and has mad gear, not all flashy and stuff. Just cool, just KJ. He lives in Compton, like the rest of us bused-in Black folk, and he has a car. As a junior, he applied to all of the big schools and scouts were constantly at the games watching him play. He and his best friend C Money had a lot of fun taking all the other cats

on the court to "b-ball school." Yeah, they schooled everybody they played with, just like Shaq and Kobe, or Iverson.

Anyway, one day right before the end of last year, KJ decided to tell my home girl, Misty, he liked me. Well, he actually said he wanted to know more about me and why I don't
hang out in South Central. Misty, the little traitor that she is,
told KJ I have identity issues, and that I'm all mixed up because I hang out with the White cats, the Puerto Rican cats,
the Samoan cats, the Mexican cats, and anybody else I feel
like hangin' with. Basically, Misty is the one with identity issues because yes, she's half Puerto Rican herself but tries to
front like she's not. I don't see what the big deal is. She's
such a hater.

But like I was saying, KJ was digging me, and I knew it,
but I also knew he was dating this senior named Maisha, and
she was known for being this tough broad who would whip
anyone who crossed her, including KJ. So, I wasn't about to
entertain the thought of talking to him, not then anyway. But
it turned out he and I went to summer school together. He
was taking some math classes and going to basketball camp.
I was taking an extra A.P. English course I needed for the fall.
Well, to make a not-so-long story even shorter, we started
dating.

C Money and two other Compton brothas usually rode to
school with KJ. Well, when KJ and I started dating, he would
pick me up in the morning too. So, there we were, four
brothas and me, rolling in KJ's little ride listening to Usher. I
was in love.

I used to watch him ball, and he was just so very fine. He
was sweet, cute, romantic, everything a first heartbreak is
supposed to be, right? To top it all off, Mama even liked him,
and his parents liked me. I thought I was in heaven.

Well, the hell started when Maisha came back from Loyola

Marymount. Apparently, her tough self got kicked out of college for talking back to her coach one too many times. So, she came back to Compton and naturally wanted KJ back. At first, she said she wanted him back as a basketball partner 'cause she played too. Whatever. She can have him because I'm through.

Back to Trecee, who wants to jump me over this same punk. She's off her rocker. Straight-up crazy. Lunatic, over this fool. She wants me to understand that KJ is her man. I say fine, understood, but me being the smart-ass that I am I ask her, in front of everyone, if Maisha knows this or what. That pisses her off even more.

Well, it goes down like this: Trecee wants to fight me right here on the first day of school, in front of all these people and with me in my new clothes. She must be crazier than I think. I'm wondering what to do. But then I spot a mutual friend of ours, Jason—an ex-con who's a little too old to be in the eleventh grade—coming down the main hall to stop Trecee before she even starts. He fights his way through the crowd that has gathered and grabs Trecee's arm.

"Let go of me, Jason. I need to teach this girl a lesson," Trecee says, struggling with Jason's grip. Her friend tries to help Trecee break free, but Jason's too strong for them.

"Come on, Trecee. Let's get your ass calm before you go to class," Jason says, leading Trecee back down the hall toward the courtyard.

"What the hell are you talking about, Trecee?" I yell to her back. "I ain't got no beef with you," I say, trying to reason with her. Whatever her response is gets swallowed up by the space between us, but I think it's something like, "Don't think this is over, Jayd. We'll have it out about you and my man."

My girls, Nellie and Mickey, are walking up the hall now.

They practically start running when they see me. The crowd of kids part to let them through.

"Hey, girl, what's going on?" Mickey asks.

"Nothing I can't handle," I say, not wanting to make a big deal out of it. People are starting to lose interest and disperse anyway.

"Is everything all right?" Nellie asks.

"Yes, everything's fine. Thanks, Nellie. You got my sweater in that cute little Gucci bag? How are you going to fit your books in that?" I ask, smiling at her silly self, as she hands me my black sweater. Nellie is my home girl, and Mickey is her home girl, making her cool by association.

"Can you believe that crazy broad wants to fight me over KJ?" I say, watching Trecee pace the courtyard back and forth like an angry bull.

"KJ?" Mickey asks confused.

I report that KJ and I have broken up. Nellie and Mickey try to console me, but I'm tired of thinking about KJ.

"Well, I guess he's with Trecee now," Nellie says.

I can't really respond to Nellie. I'm too busy trying to collect myself. Trecee caught me completely off guard. For a minute I almost went back to my hood days. Had this happened a couple years ago, I would've slapped her before she got her first earring off. But now I'm a changed sistah.

"So y'all ain't heard nothing about this? She didn't tell anybody about wanting to jump me on the first day?" Now, I don't believe this. Nobody in all of Compton knew anything about this broad wanting to fight me. No, I don't believe it.

Just then, Miss Traitor herself, Misty, walks up with a weird look on her face. "What's up, Jayd?" I knew right then she was the guilty party. She would never try to make conversation with me when I was with my girls. She would simply walk right by.

You see, me and Misty were real tight when I first came to South Bay High. There's mad history between us, even though it was only our first year. There was so much going on in both our lives and we just bonded, well, at least until she started trippin' over the summer.

We both were the new Black girls, with breasts too large for our frames. We even resembled each other in the face. In other words, she was cute too. But, there was something untrustworthy about Misty. I couldn't put my finger on it at first, but she was a trip, and I knew it from the get-go.

I have always had issues picking out best friends. I guess that's why I really don't have one now. Ever since I can remember, girls have had problems with me. For no reason at all some girls will just hate on me, and all I really wanted was to be accepted.

You see, I've always "stuck out" because of my larger-than-they-should-have-been breasts. They started to grow in elementary school and just never stopped. So, ever since junior high, dudes have been salivating over them, and me. This, of course, did not make me a favorite among the broads. I say broads because they were hating on me for something that was not under my control, and that's my definition of a sister-turned-broad, like Misty.

Misty hates me because she's jealous of the attention I get. Not from my breasts, but from my personality. She says I'm pushy and aggressive. Well, yes, I'm assertive and I don't take no crap, but that's not a reason for Misty or anyone else to hate me. For example, I just didn't let my oversized breasts stop me from being myself. Though I did get a breast reduction at the beginning of our sophomore year, that was no reason for Misty to trip. She basically said she felt betrayed. Yes, betrayed was this broad's exact wording. Like I had gotten rid of close personal friends of hers. The issues she has, I tell you. So, after the reduction, I became even more active in the Drama Club and dance, and developed a social life, which did not include Misty.

So ever since then, Misty has been trying to find sneaky, vindictive ways to be a part of my life, even if she plays the devil in it. Telling some stupid lie on me to Trecee would not be the first—or last—broadish move of Misty's to hate on me. I know she's the guilty party in this whole mess. No need to prove it. She always reveals herself in time. Just like she did today.

"Hey y'all, what happened here? Did somebody get their butt beat down or what?"

"No, Misty, but I don't doubt that's what you wanted to see. How come you weren't on the bus this morning? " I ask.

"Oh, well, I got a ride this morning," she says all nervous like she is lying to Judge Judy.

"From who?" I ask, 'cause I know her mama didn't bring her. Misty's mama, Maria, needs at least two drinks to get up in the morning, and the morning didn't start this early for her. She got demoted last year from full-time to part-time secretary because she could never make it before second period.

"Oh, um, Jason brought me to school."

"Doesn't Trecee roll with him in the morning?" Nellie asks. We call her Ms. Cleo 'cause she knows the what, when, where, why, who, and how of all the drama—and there is always plenty of it.

"If you rode with Jason and Trecee, why are you just getting here?" Mickey raises a good question.

"I had some other business to take care of. Jason can't give a sistah a ride sometimes? Damn, why y'all sweatin' me? I just came to say 'what's up,' a first day friendly gesture, but never mind now."

That broad was busted. I felt like beating Misty's lying behind right then and there, but I kept my cool. So that's how Jason knew to come stop the fight.

"Girls. Y'all always got some stuff going down," Jason says, walking back in from the courtyard where he left Trecee to calm down. "Keep me out of this. I ain't giving nobody no more rides." Jason walked away, looking pissed and slightly amused. Dudes love it when girls fight, just not when they get dragged into the middle of them.

Knowing Misty, this is only the beginning of the mess she's stirring up. She probably took the opportunity to tell every little made-up detail about me and KJ she could fester while she was in the car with Trecee. That broad can be creative when she wants to be. She needs to use that creativity of hers in English class and save all that drama she brings for Shakespeare.

You see, Misty ain't too smart when it comes to school. Or at least she doesn't apply herself. She is way too worried about being popular and in other folks' business than doing the right thing in class. She needs someone else's drama to feed from or her day is not complete.

"So, Misty, you mean to tell me the entire time you were riding with Jason and Trecee, you and she didn't talk at all?" I ask, trying to see if she would come clean.

"Look, Johnnie Cochran, I don't have to lie to you. I ain't on trial. Dang, Jayd, you always acting so suspicious of me. What have I ever done to you to make you like that?" she asks, trying to gain some sympathy from somewhere but not here.

"No you didn't just say that to me, in front of God and everybody else, Misty. What have you done to me? Oh, well let me tell you what you've done, starting with talking behind my back and backstabbing me every chance you get."

Of course the bell for first period rings right when I am on a roll. On the first day the bell rings about ten minutes later than usual. Everyone goes their separate ways, for now. Why does Misty have to start the year off so early with drama? I bet she couldn't wait to get to school this morning, I just know it.

This mess has probably been brewing all summer, and no doubt Misty has been letting Trecee simmer in her lies the entire time. She and Trecee became friends last year. Every time Misty meets somebody new, she tries to get in with them real tight, and then spin her web of deceit. I should know. She tried to make me one of her victims when I first came to Drama High.

The only teacher I can talk to at this school is Mrs. Crowe. I've never had her as a teacher, but she was my advisor last year when I was in ASB. Mrs. Crowe, or Ms. Toni as she likes her students to call her, knows about the fallout between me and Misty over the summer. I came to visit her every day during summer school, but she doesn't know about KJ and me breaking up since it only happened two days ago. I'm still in shock myself. I'll have to wait until after second period's over to talk to her at break.

10:09 A.M.

Mrs. Crowe's sitting at her desk in the back of the ASB office, which is made up of three classrooms: a main classroom where all the meetings are held; an alcove for the copier, fax machine, and computer; and a lounge area adjacent to Ms. Toni's office.

She's the only Black teacher at the school. Her husband, Mr. Crowe, was a bus driver for the Metro. Unfortunately, he died last year in a tragic accident on the 110/10 freeway exchange.

Mr. Crowe was on his normal bus route and got behind a tractor trailer carrying big steel beams. It was rush hour, so traffic must've been awful. Well, as traffic picked up pace, so did the truck, but not Mr. Crowe's bus. He knew better than to speed up too quickly on the 110/10 exchange. It's tricky and there are always way too many cars going in four different directions.

As he was sitting in traffic behind the tractor trailer, the driver of the trailer made a sudden, hard stop to avoid hitting a car. Apparently, one of the steal beams the truck was hauling was loose or at least that was the way it was told to Mrs. Crowe. She couldn't identify her husband's body because the beam came straight through the driver's side and decapitated him. It wasn't a clean cut. His face was mutilated from the broken glass caused by the shattered windshield. She could only see his left hand. She used his wedding ring to identify him.

This happened after I returned from my surgery the first semester of last year. She didn't come back to work until the end of the second semester. When Mrs. Crowe did return, she stayed in her office for the first week, not talking to anyone unless she absolutely had to. I felt sorry for her. She was so sad and I really wanted to help her, so I asked Mama what to do.

"Write her a little note to lift her spirits and give her a single yellow rose. She'll appreciate the gesture."

I did just as Mama suggested. Mrs. Crowe never acknowledged the note, but she did appreciate the rose. After that, Mrs. Crowe would always ask me to run errands for her or to help with special projects. There were only a few weeks left in the school year by then, but it was long enough for us to become each other's home away from home.

After that, Mrs. Crowe became my school Mama. She always has my back. She tells me about any and every opportunity to compete for scholarships and grants and speaking engagements, etc. Later this year, she's helping me apply to summer programs at UCLA, Long Beach State, and Cal State Northridge.

Ms. Toni kinda reminds me of a taller, slightly older version of my mom. She always has a smile on her face and people just seem to gravitate toward her. She doesn't have to do anything for her students, especially not for me. But, she does anyway. She goes out of her way to make sure I'm doing OK. When I arrive at her door, she's sitting with a cup of coffee in her hand.

"Hey, Ms. Toni." I walk around her desk to give her a big hug. It feels like she lost another pound or two from her already thin frame.

"Jayd. Girl, you look gorgeous. And those boots. You're really saying something with those, girl. How's your first day going? Misty causing any trouble yet?"

Ms. Toni is a very attractive woman and must be in her fifties, but she'll never tell. She looks like she could've been a supermodel, like Iman or Naomi Campbell, but much thinner.

I then give her the rundown on Trecee, KJ, and my suspicion of Misty's hand in all the early morning drama.

Ms. Toni lifts my chin, gives me a tissue to wipe my tears, and has a serious look on her face when she speaks to me. "Well, sweetie, as much as you might like to blame everything on the girls, remember KJ's hand is in this too. Had he been upfront and honest with you about Maisha and Trecee from the beginning, there would be no room for this kind of mess. KJ's the person you have a problem with. Focus on getting this straight with him and hopefully the bull with the girls will work itself out."

She's right. All KJ had to do was tell the truth and things might not be so twisted now. KJ could've been more honest with me through our entire relationship. But no, he just couldn't let me know what he was doing before all this blew up in my face. That would've been too much like doing the right thing, I guess.

~ 7 ~
Let Me Know

*"If you ever feel the need to wonder why
Let me know."*

—AALIYAH

The main problem between me and KJ is communication. He tries to communicate his player BS to me, and I communicate back that he's full of himself. That's why we started arguing in the first place.

His super large ego is another reason we don't really get along that well. It's bigger than any I've ever seen before. This brotha thinks he's the king of kings in the flesh and that all women should bow before his majesty. I tell you, he's too much for me most of the time.

The real problems began when he started mistreating me. Brothas always treat me real nice in the beginning, but then they get comfortable. They start feeling like I owe them something. And that something is always the cookies.

Well, I'm not ready to give up my virginity anytime soon, especially not because he's picked me up from work a few times. What the hell? KJ also thinks I should feel blessed and honored to give it up to him, because so many other girls want to have the chance.

KJ would ask all the time, "When you gone stop playing hard to get and give it up, Jayd? Why you being such a goody-goody, huh, Jayd? You know how many broads want to get at this?" and on and on and on. I heard this madness for two months. Nellie thought I did the right thing by making KJ wait. Mickey, on the other hand, thought I was crazy.

"Jayd, that brotha is fine. You better jump on that."

"It's not that simple, Mickey."

"You lucky he waited this long for you. Most cats would've been out weeks ago."

I didn't want to admit it at the time, but she was right. Now I wonder if he was getting some from Trecee or Maisha on the side all along. I should have known something was up when he stopped picking me up after work. It used to be no problem, and then all of a sudden he couldn't do it anymore. No explanation, just some lie about having to work later than normal.

I found out it was a lie when my auntie Sonia picked me up from work one night. We stopped by his job because I wanted to surprise him. Of course, he wasn't there. His manager said his shift never changed. It was the same as it had always been.

I confronted him about his little lie on the phone that night and he accused me of checking up on him. This was our first big argument.

"I ain't used to no girl checking up on me, Jayd."

"I wasn't checking up on you, KJ. You just happened to get caught in a lie and now you're trying to twist this mess around on me, and I'm not having it." I was so pissed at him, I almost threw the phone against the wall.

"Jayd, I never told you I was working late tonight. You assumed I was and went hunting me down like some crazy woman," KJ says, lying through his pretty teeth.

"You're lying, KJ, and you know it, God knows it, and I know it. Ya mama probably knows it too. Who do you think I am? Some silly little broad with selective amnesia? I only remember you saying that you couldn't pick me up from work anymore in your trifling bucket of a car because your

lying butt had to work late from now on. Isn't that what you said to me?"

At that moment, I could only hear breathing over the phone. KJ was completely silent and I was on a roll.

"So, let me ask you, KJ. Why you gotta lie, huh? People only lie when they're afraid of something or someone. What are you afraid of? Just let me know so we can move on, because this is too much madness for me."

"I ain't afraid of nothing and no one. You're just too high maintenance. You expect too much from me, like all this checking up on me business . . ." I had to cut him off in the middle of his twisted player ill-logic and check his lie.

"Excuse me, KJ, but how is accepting an offer made by my boyfriend to pick me up from work being high maintenance? Break that one down for me, please. You're straight tripping on this phone tonight, KJ. I don't know what has gotten in to you, but I sure do hope you return to normal soon, because this side of you is not pretty to me at all."

"Jayd, you expect a brotha to do all of this stuff for you, yet I get nothing in return. Why should I go out of my way to show my love when you won't go out of your way to show me yours?"

Yes, he did try to use that twisted player bull logic on me. He must have forgotten temporarily who I am, because normally he wouldn't have said something so stupid to me.

"KJ, I think you have completely lost your mind, 'cause you should know a hell of a lot better than to say some stupid mess like that to me. You know my cookies ain't for sale . . . not for free rides from work, dinner, or anything else. And on that note, I will see you at school tomorrow, or have I lost my ride to summer school too? Maybe by tomorrow you'll be back to the normal KJ that I know and love." And just like that, I hung up the phone.

* * *

"Girl, no he didn't lie to you? My mama always said that men ain't nothing but lying, cheating bastards and that they're all Satan's soldiers." I told you that Misty's mom was messed up.

"Well, I wouldn't say all that, but I don't appreciate his lying, and then to say that it's my fault because I won't give it up. Let me know if I'm being unreasonable, but damn, he's really trippin', huh, Misty?"

Now usually, Misty would have my back no matter who we would be talking about. But, on this one she sighed and said, *"Well, Jayd, y'all have been going out for a couple of months and he does treat you nice, and he's KJ. Why you don't want to give it up to him? You said he told you he loved you, and I know you love him. So, what's the problem?"*

I didn't have an answer for her that night. I didn't know why I didn't want to have sex with KJ. I just didn't feel it was the right time, ya know? I can't explain it. I did love him and he did get me all excited and stuff, but sex? Too big, too soon. I didn't know if I was ready.

Then I made the mistake of telling Misty I might have sex with KJ at some point in the future. She of course went back and told KJ this, and he started acting all sweet and nice again. She didn't tell me she told him about our conversation, so I thought KJ had come around to my way of thinking. Man, was I wrong.

One night after a summer football game in El Segundo, KJ asked me to go to the beach with him. Even though I was staying at my mom's house, I knew I still had to call Mama to ask if it was okay. She said cool. "Just don't stay out too late or come back pregnant." Mama always knows what to say and when.

KJ and I are having a nice time at the beach, when he starts kissing me real hard. I hate when he does that.

"Damn, KJ, why you kissing me like that? This ain't One Life to Live.*"*

"I'm sorry, Jayd. It's just that you taste so good, I want to make sure I get all of you."

This did not sound like KJ at all. It sounded like his older basketball cronies. Not this mess again. But, just as I'm about to tell him where to go, our song "Let Me Know," by Aaliyah, comes on; we just stop to listen.

"I love this song," I say, *momentarily forgetting I'm irritated with KJ.*

"Remember our first date, KJ? You came to my house, met Mama, ate the entire plate of food she fixed you, and then asked for more?"

"Your grandmother is the best cook. I need to drop by soon to grub, and say hi to Mama, of course."

KJ has a genuine affection for Mama. I think because his grandparents live out of state, he misses having a grandparent around. I've noticed he really likes older people. Even when he's at work old women are always talking to him and saying how sweet and cute he is. If they only knew he was an angel in disguise.

"You know I love you, right, KJ?"

"Yeah, I know. So why don't you let me know what's up with the games, Jayd? You acting like you don't want to, but I know you do. So why don't you just cut out the act and let's get down to it," KJ said, *trying to pull me closer to him.* I guess he thought the song plus his weak little line was supposed to make me say "Okay, Your Majesty" and bow down. I don't think so.

"Whatever gave you the idea I was playing come and get it games with you, fool? I've been straight up about this whole thing from day one. I said I wasn't ready. I ain't ready. And I don't think I'll ever be ready to with you," I say.

"Well, that ain't what your girl said."

"What girl?" Now I was on red-level-pissed-off-in-a-serious-way mode.

"Misty said you really want to get with this, but you're just afraid. Don't be mad, Jayd; she was just trying to help me out. I been trying to figure you out, and I can't. Sometimes it seems like you want to, but then you always say no . . ."

"That's because I mean NO!" I shout in KJ's face. "Take me home now so I can call Misty and cuss her out. And, thank you for showing me I can't trust you or her anymore. How dare you two plot when, how, and to whom I'll give up my cookies. How you know I want to give it up to you anyway? I never told you that. You don't listen, KJ. That's your problem. You just can't believe someone don't want to sleep with your conceited self. Well, I'm here to let you know there's at least one girl who doesn't and won't. Maybe you and Misty should get together, since y'all seem to have it all worked out."

"Jayd, don't be like that . . ."

"Take me home now, KJ. I'm through talking to you for the night."

That was our last date. Since we were closer to Mama's than my mom's house, I made him take me there. As soon as I walked through my front door, I got the phone from the hallway table and stormed outside onto the front porch. I wanted to make sure I was out of earshot when I told off Misty. There are too many nosey folks around my house.

She picked up on the first ring.

"What's up, Misty?"

"Jayd, what you doing home this early? I thought you went out with KJ tonight?"

"I did. But it seems KJ was on the wrong date. He thought

he was on a date with the Jayd who wanted to give it up because her best friend told him so. Do you know that Jayd? Because next time you need to send her on the date, not me."

"Girl, you so silly," Misty laughs. "So, tell me what happened. Was it all romantic and stuff?"

I can tell Misty is confused. She really doesn't know how to respond because she can't tell just how pissed I am yet.

"Nothing happened. How could you tell that fool I wanted to sleep with him? What gave you the right to decide when, where, and who I give up MY cookies to?" Misty is silent. Now she's getting the picture and I am getting hotter and hotter as the minutes pass by.

Finally, she's got something to say. "Jayd, stop trippin'. The other night on the phone you sounded like you wanted to but were just scared to tell him. So, being the good friend that I am, I just did it for you. What's the big deal?"

"The big deal is that you betrayed my trust. I was talking to you, not him, Miss National Inquirer. If I had wanted him to know I would have told him. It's not your place to tell anybody a thing I talk to you about, or don't you know how to be a best friend?"

"You know what, Jayd? You don't deserve KJ. All this drama you creating over nothing but an opportunity to get with the finest brotha at school, and you want to jump down my throat for trying to make it happen. I could be like them other broads that be hatin' on you, tryin' to get with your man. But no, I try to help and this is the thanks I get."

"Help? How in the hell did you try to help me? By going behind my back and telling him our private conversation? Yeah, thanks for the help, Misty. With a friend like you, I don't need broads hatin' on me."

"Oh, see, now you're being too dramatic for me. That's the last time I help you out."

"Thank you. 'Cause like I've told you before, I don't need your help when it comes to my love life."

"That's the point, you don't have one."

"Neither do you. But, unlike you, I don't want one just yet."

"Yeah, but KJ does." I ignored that little comment then. But now I see I shouldn't have. She knew about Trecee and Maisha all along. And then she went there. To that unforgivable place in any sistahood where the line is crossed to the point of no return.

"You just a stupid little ho, Jayd. You think you too damn good for everybody. I tried to be your friend, but forget you. You ain't normal and I'm tired of defending you. I'm not spending a new school year dealing with your weird self."

"Did you just call me a ho? You know what, Misty, I'll handle your ass at school. You can't call me no names and get away with it."

Since Misty didn't finish summer school, and I was working hard trying to finish with a good grade, I didn't see or talk to her again until today. I can't believe this. First this broad trips on me after my breast reduction, telling everybody about my surgery after I told her I didn't want anyone to know. I forgave her then, but now this. Misty gets jealous and it just blinds her. With friends like her, I don't need any more enemies.

I'd never felt as hurt or betrayed by anyone as I did by Misty that night. I've learned the hard way you just can't trust everybody. It seems to me the people I trust the most always end up the ones causing me the most pain.

After my argument with Misty, I sat outside smelling the crisp night air, listening to the neighbors watching reruns of *Good Times.* Mama's dog Lexi pushed open the back gate and sat next to me on the porch. I swear sometimes I feel like she's the only one I can truly trust—besides Mama, that is.

3:30 P.M.

I'm so glad I get through the rest of the day without seeing anyone, especially KJ. I want to avoid him for as long as possible. I'm so ready to go home, I drop off my schedule to Mr. Adelezi and head straight to the bus stop without saying good-bye to Nellie and Mickey; they'd just try to convince me to hang out after school.

On the way to the bus stop, I see Jeremy, this White boy who makes me feel all funny inside, getting into his '66 Mustang with a mutual friend of ours, Chance. Damn he's fine.

As he walks around to the driver's side of his car, I notice how even-toned his olive complexion is. The afternoon sun hits his hazel eyes at an angle that makes them shimmer like cat eyes. He's hairy, but it only complements his trim, muscular body. He wears his usual outfit: a T-shirt, basketball shorts, and Birkenstocks on his feet.

"Hey, Jayd," Chance says, crossing the street to greet me.

"Hey, Chance. How was your summer?" I ask while reaching out to give him a bear hug.

"It was great. I missed you at the beach. What did you get into?" he asks. I instantly think of Simply Wholesome, KJ, my mom's house, and the drive-by. I decide to go with the obvious answer.

"I was working," I say, sneaking a peek at Jeremy, still standing at his car.

"Have you met my boy Jeremy?" Chance asks, seeing my obvious jocking through my fake Louis Vuitton shades.

"Yeah, we've met. I actually have a class with him this semester and . . ." Before I could finish my thought, Chance yells to Jeremy to come and join us. He can be such a jerk sometimes. But, I love him like the White brother I never thought I'd have. As Jeremy walks over, I can feel the heat rise from my body to my face. I hope this boy doesn't notice my blushing.

"Jeremy, you met my girl Jayd, right?" Chance asks, pulling me close to him, just like a big brother would.

"Yeah, in Government class," he says, letting his smile get as big as mine must be right about now. "How's it going, Jayd?" he asks.

"It's going," I say, instantly feeling embarrassed. Why'd I have to say that?

"Isn't she the cutest little thing you've ever seen?" Chance says, rubbing my head.

"Fool, would you cut it out? You gone mess up my braids," I say, jerking away from his embrace.

"How was your summer?" Jeremy asks, actually looking interested in my response.

"Too short," I say, still surprised that this boy is talking to me. "And yours?" I ask, returning the interest.

"It was cool. Surfing and all that. You know, the usual," Jeremy says, looking from me to Chance, like he's trying to figure out our relationship. "So, how do you know this loser?" he says, punching Chance in the arm.

"Watch it, man. I just finished working out. You're liable to break your hand on these rocks, baby," Chance says, flexing his limp biceps in the air.

"We're in the Drama Club. And, he just kind of attached himself to me over the past year," I say, smacking his arm out of the air. He's such a damn fool.

"You know you love it, baby," Chance says, embracing me in another bear hug and picking me up.

"Put me down!" I scream. Jeremy's just watching and laughing at us.

"Dude, put her down and stop playing around. We got business to handle," Jeremy says, looking down at his ringing cell phone. I like this old-school ring tone. It reminds me of the antique rotary phone we still use in Mama's room.

"Chance, sometimes you play too much," I say, straightening out my clothes and catching my breath.

"All right lets go. Jayd, we'll see your fine self tomorrow," Chance says, walking back over to Jeremy's car.

"Yeah, we'll talk in class tomorrow, Jayd," Jeremy says as he heads back to his car, leaving me anxious to wake up the next morning. For the first time today, I'm actually looking forward to the rest of the school year.

"See y'all tomorrow," I say, walking toward the bus stop. As they speed off toward the beach, I wonder what kind of trouble they're about to get into. I hope my bus ride is uneventful. I need the rest of the day to be peaceful, especially if I'm going to get all this homework done. I hope the vibe at home is laid-back too.

~ 8 ~
Women's Work

"Baby check yourself, brace yourself
Protect yourself, face yourself."

—ERYKAH BADU

When I come home from school I like to immediately change out of my clothes, eat some hot Chee-tos or some Poli Seeds, and chill out listening to my portable CD player. I walk in the back door and notice Jay sitting on the couch. Instead of doing his homework, he's watching TV.

"Jay, why you ain't doing your homework?" I ask, walking past him and into Mama's room.

"I ain't got no homework. It's the first week of school," Jay yells from the living room.

"How you gone be a senior and I got more homework than you?" I say, already knowing his response.

"That's because you go to that White-ass school. You see, if they put you over there with me at Compton, you wouldn't have no homework this week and you could chill and watch videos."

I come out of the room just to look at his stupid self.

"Jay, that's not true. Plenty of students at Compton got homework today, I'm sure. Your lazy butt just ain't doin' it."

I go into Daddy's room to get my clothes out of the closet and see Bryan knocked out on his bed. I dig down to the bottom of my clothes bag and pull out a Bebe shirt, some jean shorts, and my CD player. I take my stuff back into Mama's room and get comfortable. Unlike Jay, I have a grip of home-work tonight.

"If the phone rings, answer it, please. I'm expecting Nellie to call," I shout at Jay from the room.

"What I look like, your secretary?" he yells back.

"Just answer the phone, fool," I say while opening my math book, but my concentration is quickly broken by the ringing phone.

"Jayd, pick up the phone," Jay yells.

I put my books down and walk over to Mama's side of the room. She keeps her phone well hidden under her bed.

"Hello?"

"What's up, Jayd?" Mickey asks. I can hear all of her brothers and sisters in the background. She has six siblings, so her house is always noisy. Nellie's on the phone too.

"Hey, girl. We're just checking on you," Nellie says. "You left school without saying a word."

"I know. I'm sorry. I just had to get home. Did I miss any-thing?"

"Girl, when you left that broad was talking about jumping you," Nellie blurts out. "She said she gone get you the first chance she gets."

"Are you serious, Nellie?" I ask, dumbfounded. This is hap-pening on the first day of school. What did I do to deserve this?

"Girl, hell yes," Nellie says.

"Trecee is on one, Jayd," Mickey chimes in. "What did KJ put on her? You shoulda got some of that while you had the chance," Mickey continues, only half-joking.

"Mickey, what's wrong with you?" Nellie says, pretending to be offended. "That man is obviously damaged goods be-cause the broads he's with are crazy after being with him."

"Yeah," Mickey admits, "but you got to give it to him on this: He must have some kind of loving to get girls this sprung on him."

"Mickey, damn!" I yell. "You can be so crass at times. Are you really that curious about KJ?" I ask. Now I'm getting pissed. "Everybody just loves KJ. He ain't that great or fine or whatever. And, believe me, the brotha's got a thing or two to learn about giving as well as receiving," I say, temporarily shutting Mickey up. "I got to go."

"Ah, hell nah, Jayd. What did you mean by that? He's got a thing to learn about giving what?" Mickey asks.

"I'll see you tomorrow. I'm too tired to finish this conversation."

"Jayd, what you and KJ do? You always acting so damn innocent. See, I knew you were a freak," Mickey says.

"All I'm saying is that KJ has no patience and no respect. If we were to do anything, it would be all for his benefit and that's not the way it should be."

"That's right, Jayd," Nellie says.

"Whatever. I still think you shoulda got with that when you had the chance," Mickey says, not relenting.

"Whatever, Mickey." I'm trying not to sound too irritated with her, but she can work my nerves sometimes.

"Mickey and I are going to the mall after school tomorrow. You down?" Nellie asks, cleverly changing the subject. She can tell when I've had enough of Mickey for one day.

"Yeah, I'm down," I answer. I could use some new sandals. It's too hot to be wearing boots or Nikes every day.

"And, Jayd, don't worry about that girl. Ain't nothing gone happen tomorrow. She'd be a fool to try something again," Nellie says, trying to reassure me.

"I'm not worried about her trying something. I'm worried about her making me do something I don't want to do."

"What's that?" Nellie asks.

"Defend myself." I haven't really had a fight since I've been at South Bay High. Me and Misty have cat fights every now and then, but an all-out brawl? No, not yet. The last time I had one of those was in junior high, and I sent that girl to the hospital.

"Well, for her sake I hope she's just playing around," Nellie says. She knows how wild I can get when pushed. She's only witnessed me going off on Misty a time or two, but that's enough to make her never want to see me fight someone.

"Yeah, well I just can't wait for this to all come to an end. See you tomorrow, chicas," I say.

"Toodles," Nellie says in her usual upbeat way.

"Later, Jayd."

"Later, Mickey."

After I hang up the phone, I hear Mama and Jay talking in the living room. Mama walks in the bedroom with her purse on her shoulder and shopping bags in tow.

"What was all that about defending yourself?" Mama asks. I swear she's got the hearing of a wolf.

Maybe Mama can help me solve some of the drama at school. "Mama, can you give me a potion to keep crazy people away from me or teach me how to put a curse on someone?" I ask.

"Now, Jayd, you know that's not how we work," she says, putting her shopping bags into her closet.

"What happened to the charm bag I gave you this morning?" Mama asks while changing clothes. She takes off her red slacks and panty hose, carefully hanging them both on a wire hanger and putting them in the closet. There's hardly any room in there for another hanger, but somehow she makes it fit.

I forgot all about my No More Drama charm bag. I put it in my backpack this morning and haven't seen it since. I put my homework down and grab my backpack from the foot of my bed.

"I think I put it in my pencil bag," I say, opening the side pocket.

Mama stops undressing and shakes her head, taking a long, deep sigh. "Jayd, I told you to put that bag in your purse and now you don't know where it is," Mama says, sounding disappointed.

"I didn't lose it," I say, frantically searching for the charm bag. What did I do with it? It's go to be in here somewhere.

"Jayd, you've got to take your lessons more seriously," she says, continuing to take off her cream blouse and shell. Mama takes her yellow housedress off a nail hanging in the closet and puts it on over her head without moving a single hair out of place.

"How are you going to ask for more help when you don't take the help I already gave you seriously?" Obviously irritated, Mama grabs some white towels and T-shirts from the top shelf of the closet. She puts them down on the bed, walks over to her nightstand, and picks up her journal.

"Every time a client asks for my help, I write down their question, the answer, the work prescribed to help them with their problem, and the final outcome. Over half of my clients come back to me repeatedly for the same thing." Mama stops turning the fragile pages of her journal and reads silently to herself. I dare not say a word.

"When they come back, I ask if they've completed whatever work I gave them to do with their last consultation. More often than not, the answer is no. And so, I give them the same work to do over again until it is done." She puts the journal down, rubs her forehead, and continues. "I don't give you work to do because I want to punish you, Jayd. I give it to you because I want to help you and teach you how to help yourself and eventually others. You must have faith in what you already have before you go off looking for answers in curses and potions."

Now I feel like crap. Mama's right. She always is. I stop looking for the charm bag and watch Mama pick up the towels and T-shirts, along with some candles and her other spirit tools.

"We have to make the offering to Oshune now. She's your main deity and she'll handle all your problems, no matter the cause. Go into the bathroom. We're going to give you a cleansing first," Mama says without any further explanation.

Mama taught me how to give cleansing baths when I started my period. I guess it was some sort of right of passage.

First, depending on the type of cleansing, I have to boil the ingredients together in a big stainless-steel pot. Then, I have to say some prayers and prepare the bath.

The bath usually consists of things that make you smell and feel good: perfume, flowers, oils, wine (if you're old enough), and candles everywhere. Mama makes all the preparations, so I don't know what this cleansing is for. But, judging by the white, blue, and yellow candles everywhere, I'm guessing it's for protection, peace, and attraction.

I walk into the bathroom and Mama closes the door behind me; there's no room to move.

"Take off your clothes and get in the tub," Mama says, setting a big pot full of the cleansing brew down on the corner of the tub. She begins to pour the contents into the tub while running cold water.

"Hey. Who's in the bathroom?" Carl asks, banging on the door.

"Carl, go away. We're busy," Mama shouts.

"We? Ah damn, are y'all doing another cleansing? People got to shit, you know?" Carl says, walking away from the bathroom door.

Mama hands me the pot and tells me to keep pouring. Mama opens the bathroom door and yells out to anybody who can hear, "The next person who bangs on this door or makes any unnecessary noise while we're in here is going to get a cast-iron skillet up their head." Without another word, Mama closes the bathroom door and continues to mix the contents in the tub.

I finish pouring everything into the tub and indulge in fragrances that overwhelm me. The candle's light calms me and makes everything in the dingy little bathroom seem to glow.

"Mama, why do I have to do this right now? I'm tired and I've got a lot of homework to do," I say as I start to get out of the tub.

"Jayd girl, hush. You know better than to talk in the middle of a cleansing. Here, take the cup. You know what to do," Mama says, testing my basic knowledge.

I pour the brew over my head several times while reciting a prayer to my deity. The first time I did this I felt a little weird. But it works. A cleansing of any type is a really good way to calm down in this crazy world.

After the cleansing bath, Mama makes an offering to Oshune, the Yoruba deity of love, wealth, and healing. She prays for me to have the sweetness of Oshune to help me win over my enemies.

"Oshune is also a warrior, Jayd. So, don't let anyone scare you," Mama says as I step out of the tub and she steers me to the mirror. She dries me off with the white towel as I stare at my reflection. "You are blessed by both her strength and her sweetness."

Mama hands me a white gown and tells me to put it on. "You have a lot of negative energy around you at school," Mama says while draining the tub. "You have a lot of work to do to keep this mess off you. There's much more going on here than you know."

"What else is it, Mama?" I ask, turning toward her and feeling more frightened than I was by the prospect of a fight with Trecee.

"What did I say? No fear, Jayd," Mama says, pushing my chin up and forcing my intense stare back into the mirror.

"Everything will be revealed in time, child. But the drama going on with KJ and Misty ain't got nothing to do with you. So, you just need to be aware of your energy and keep as far away from the girl as you can until this is all solved," Mama says while picking up the flowers and herbs from the bottom of the empty tub.

Mama opens the bathroom door and hurries out, carrying her pot and the extinguished candles. She returns to lead me back to her room and hands me a list with assignments on it.

"This is your homework for the next two weeks. You'll be tested on it next Sunday evening," Mama says. "Pay attention while doing your assignments; don't just do it to get it done, learn something," she says, referring to the list.

I unfold the yellow parchment paper with Mama's careful and neat handwriting on it. I read the list to myself. It's more prayers, poems, and stories about the different deities.

"Mama, why I got to do all this work? I've got too much on my mind to be doing all this right now," I complain. All I asked for was a little help. Not a list of more stuff to do.

"Your petty little drama at school ain't nothing compared to the drama out here in the real world. Tell that to them little heffas stirring up all this mess behind you and KJ. Now, go get Mama some water so I can take my herbs."

As usual, Mama's right. I shouldn't be worrying about this drama when there are so many more important things to think about. But still, Trecee and KJ will be on my mind all night long.

When I walk back into Mama's room to hand her her herbs and get my backpack to take into the kitchen—I still have schoolwork to do—Mama's already asleep on her bed. In her hand lay a Bible and her rosary. I hope she prayed for Trecee to chill the hell out. I pray the cleansing works. I need as much protection and good vibes around me as possible. Mama doesn't play games when it comes to my safety or my heart. I wish everybody felt the same way.

~ 9 ~
Games

"Girl, you know you better watch out
Some guys, some guys are only about that thing."

—LAURYN HILL

This triangle with KJ and Trecee is like a bad soap opera, but not like *The Young and the Restless* or *General Hospital*. This is more like some *OC* type drama. Just straight out of nowhere and ridiculous.

The games they play on the soaps are some of the most twisted and wicked I've ever seen. Maybe Trecee is headed for a successful career as a writer for the soaps because I don't know that even they could have come up with a more ludicrous plot.

But she's not the only one playing games. KJ has his player scent all over this broad. He's got her all twisted up like a dreadlock. And now she's out of control. He got this broad thinking she's his girl when everybody knows he's just playing her. Trecee's way out her league with KJ. How she could be that blind, I don't know. But obviously she's willing to fight for him no matter how foolish he makes her look. I hope she doesn't follow us to the mall. It's Back to School Night tonight, so we get out of school early, which gives me some well-deserved chill time with my girls.

"Hey, y'all want to catch a movie? Wednesdays are half off," Mickey says.

"Girl, we ain't got time for all that. We're going to miss all the new cats hangin' out at the food court. You know broads be quick to flock." Nellie is so boy crazy sometimes.

"Ain't nobody looking for a new man, Nellie." I say. "Why are we always concentrating on getting dudes anyway? New ones, old ones, it doesn't matter. They're all dogs."

"Ah, sweetie," Nellie says. "It sounds like you just got your heart broken by a fine ass Black man. You need to call Dr. Phil to get a new outlook."

"Nellie, you're so silly," Mickey laughs.

I have to crack a smile too.

"Besides," Mickey continues. "My man ain't no dog. He got girls jockin' him all day. But he know that what's here is much better than anything else out there." Mickey points to all the females around us. South Bay Galleria is the after-school hangout for all the schools in this area. So, not only do we get to see new dudes from our school, but also from the other schools around here.

"Yeah, but how you know he ain't got a little something on the side?" Nellie asks as Mickey reaches into her Louis Vuitton bag to get her cell phone.

"Because I keep him too happy to mess around. Besides, how you know I ain't got a little something on the side?" Mickey has dudes jockin' her all the time. And with her cute little brown-skin self, I'm sure she can have her pick of the litter at all times. "Jayd, don't be so cynical. All men ain't dogs. You just have to learn to play the game to your advantage," Mickey says, scrolling in her phone book. "I'm going to find you a rebound boyfriend."

"Mickey, what's wrong with you?" Nellie asks. "A rebound boyfriend is the last thing she needs."

"Excuse me? What the hell is a rebound boyfriend?" I ask.

"A dude to help you get over one boyfriend and on to the next one," Mickey says like it's the most normal conversation to be having.

"Mickey, no thank you. And besides, what are you going to do? Call up someone on your reject list to help me out?"

"Of course not. This list is strictly for side business. I've got some dudes on here that will make you forget all about KJ. It's all part of the game, baby," Mickey says, continuing to scroll down her little phone list while Nellie and I look for something to eat. The mall is packed with broads and dudes. Everybody's on cell phones and scouting the fresh meat at the same time. The games have just begun.

Sometimes, even I, Jayd Jackson, play games with boys. Unfortunately, I don't realize I'm playing a game until I'm smack dab in the middle of it. Now, the boys are the professional game players and hustlers. They know how to win at them all: the "oh baby, that's just my ex-girlfriend" game; the "I'm always broke" game; the "love-hate-jealousy can't stand you but I can't live without you" game; the "I don't want to admit I made a wrong decision so I'm going to make the breakup about something else" game; and the "she's just a friend" game, just to name a few.

I haven't played them all, but I've been played in a couple. I learned all about the games from this dude I used to work with, Sid. He was much, much older than me, but only dated girls my age or a couple of years older, at the most. He had these girls doing damn near everything he wanted. Paying his bills, putting gas in his car, and buying him stuff. He was the Mac. And to top it off, the girls knew he had other females, but they didn't care. As long as they got a little piece of him they were happy. I guess they thought they would eventually convince him to be only their man.

But, unfortunately for them broads, dude wasn't interested in having one woman. His game was rock solid and he knew it. Them broads would fight one another over him, but never him. Watching him was kinda like watching a Snoop video. He just knew he was a straight-up pimp.

* * *

"Girl, these cats are looking pretty good up in here. I'm so glad we came to the mall today," Mickey says while giving about ten different dudes her sexiest look.

"Mickey, I'm gone tell your man you out here scouting for new territory," Nellie says as we walk toward Hot Dog on a Stick.

"Ain't nobody scouting for nothing, Nellie," Mickey says, ending her hunt on my behalf to pursue her own prey. "I'm just observing the new merchandise."

"Whatever, Mickey. Relationships are sacred. I don't even see why you have a man," Nellie says, rolling her eyes at Mickey. Mickey rolls her eyes right back. "Jayd, you want a cheese on a stick and lemonade? We can share some fries," Nellie says, taking her wallet out of her Dooney & Burke bag.

"I'm really not in the mood to eat, girls. I'm tired. Mama had me up last night doing a cleansing," I say, remembering yesterday's drama.

Nellie studies the five-item menu like they added something new. Even if they did she gets the same thing every time: sugar-free lemonade, no ice, and a small fries, no salt.

"Why are you reading the menu when you already know what you want?" I ask impatiently.

"I'm tired of eating here. Let's go to Cheesecake Factory. It's only a few minutes away and they have really good food," Nellie says, temporarily forgetting who she's with.

"Nellie, ain't nobody got Cheesecake Factory money," I say, nudging her in the shoulder. I love Nellie, but she thinks she is better than us regular folk sometimes because her family got a little more money than the average folks in Compton. But not enough to live with the rich people they want to be like so bad.

"You ain't got to get all sensitive, Jayd. Avoiding Trecee

and KJ all day must have you pretty tired," she says, trying to be funny.

"Ain't nobody avoiding stupid KJ or Trecee, Nellie. I just needed some time to myself," I say, lying through my teeth. Ever since my cleansing last night I've been thinking about what Mama said: This drama ain't mine and to stay as far away from Trecee as possible.

"Yeah, right, Jayd," Nellie says, standing in line for her lemonade. "That's why you stayed in Mrs. Crowe's office during break and lunch. It's only the second day of school and you're already in hiding."

"If I was you, I'd just kick Trecee's butt and get on with it. You can take her," Mickey says while counting her money.

After we get our food and drinks, we sit at a table in the big open quad area in the center of the food court. We choose to sit by The Sweet Factory because it smells so good.

"You know what? Both of y'all can just stay out of my business. I'm not avoiding Trecee or KJ," I reiterate.

"Well, since you ain't avoiding nobody, why don't you go tell your boy we said, 'Hi,'" Nellie says, pointing to KJ and his crew.

And, there he is, ordering a slice of pizza at Napoli's, looking like a movie star. I swear that boy is the finest Black dude I've ever seen. Maybe Misty was right. What the hell? Did I just think that? I must be momentarily blinded by his immaculate smile and even-toned brown skin. He towers over everyone else in his crew with his six-foot two-inch frame. He's muscular and lean, just perfect for me, and every other female in this mall.

KJ and his crew like to dress in all the latest sports fashion. He always wears Nike and Sean Jean sweats and shirts with the shoes to match. On a sunny day, the visor is in effect, and it highlights his narrow face and high cheekbones that light up when he smiles. He's beautiful.

"I can't believe he's up here hangin' out like nothing's happening," I say. I hate that this dude can get broads to create all kinds of drama over him while he's seemingly untouched by the insanity swirling around him.

"Well, ain't you doing the same thing?' Mickey says, not missing eye contact with a single dude who walks by. She loves getting attention from as many cats as she can.

"No, I'm not," I say, pretending to be hurt. "I'm here for some serious rehabilitation that only the mall can provide. And that jerk is ruining my vibe."

"Well, the other girls swarming around him don't seem to mind his vibe at all." I see that Nellie's right. KJ is good at what he does best in all scenarios: playing.

KJ's a true player. I think he learned how to master the game from some of the older brothers he balls with. Them brothas are from UCLA and USC, and they all love high school girls. Not just because we're young, sweet, and fine, but also because most of us fall for the game. They know this too, so they're always hangin' around the mall, usually Fox Hills, where all the fly girls chill.

Getting into this older crew is a guaranteed ticket into the game. You see, games can't be played alone. Not these kind. Players need "their boys" to back them up, make sure their game is tight, you know the deal. So, if they have a crew, they're halfway there.

Anyway, KJ and his crew are the b-ball brothas and their game is airtight like Iverson's. Iverson is so beautiful. But yeah, that brotha got airtight games goin' on, and he learned it all from his older crew. What he learns from them he takes back to C Money and Del, trying to hip them to the game. So, you can imagine that KJ's not only "The Man" to girls, but the guys also look up to KJ for his so-called player wisdom.

Well, the "oh-so-wise-one" first pulled his player wisdom on Maisha but she flipped the script on him. He learned a very quick lesson: Girls can be players too. Turns out the reason they broke up the first time was because Maisha was dating one of KJ's crew without either of them knowing. Major game violation. Anyhow, Maisha got to talkin' one day and mentioned this other brotha's name to one of her friends, who was of course hating on Maisha. (Every sistah has a broad or two hating on them in their life.)

Word eventually got back to Mr. Playa himself and he confronted Maisha. Well, she fessed up to the whole thing and then asked KJ why he made such a big deal about it? Yeah, she twisted his whole mind up. Maisha doesn't just play the game; she masters it to her advantage. She quit KJ for the other brotha, and that's where I came in.

KJ decided on me as his next victim, or woman, as he calls it. I was so awestruck by the brother I fell right into his little trap without a moment's thought as to his true intentions. Truth be told, from the first time I saw KJ I was in love.

Everything began real sweet with us. He was a perfect gentleman. He opened doors for me, took me to lunch, called me all the time, and asked before he kissed me. You know the kind of stuff that only happens in the movies? That was how his game began.

It wasn't until he had me whipped that he began to show his true player side, constantly pressuring me to give up the cookies. I wasn't having it though. I guess Trecee doesn't mind that side of him, but I do.

As KJ takes his order to a seat nearby the pizza shop he glances my way and we make eye contact. At first he looks like he's been caught with his pants down. Then, he just gives me one of his sly smiles and goes back to charming the harem closely following at his heels. Mickey and Nellie catch the eye contact.

"Jayd, why you just sitting there?" Mickey accuses. "Go over and tell that fool what you really think of him."

I shrug at her.

"Well, I'm gone get some candy. Y'all want something?" Mickey says while getting up.

"Damn, Mickey, you just had two dogs, some fries, and a large lemonade. What's up, you pregnant or something?" I ask, half teasing and half serious.

"Nah, but you know I started the patch this week and it's making me hungrier than usual. My sister says it works better than the pill. So, if I have to gain a couple of pounds, so be it. But maybe you're right; I'll pass on the sweets."

"If you ask me, all that stuff is dangerous. You should just use condoms, like other responsible people," Nellie says.

"Everybody don't like it like that. Right, Jayd?"

"What the hell you asking me for, or have you forgotten I'm a virgin?" I ask Mickey, shocked that she'd even say anything like that to me.

"I know. But you and KJ never discussed birth control?" Nellie asks, sounding like a damn family planning commercial. "Unlike Mickey's method, condoms are the only way to go, if you choose to do it at all," she says.

"Even if I intended to do it with him, he's been around way too much to be going raw. KJ said when the time came he would pull out, said it always works for him," I say, temporarily remembering our sex talk. KJ was so sweet at the beginning of our relationship. He seemed so patient, but that all went to hell quickly.

"Yeah, but that don't help with catching the stuff that will make your cookies crumble. You need to use a condom—always," Nellie says. She can act like somebody's mama sometimes.

"It ain't like she really got to worry about it, Nellie. There are plenty of broads flocking over to KJ and his boys. Just look," Mickey says, pointing to the crowd surrounding KJ, Dell, and C Money.

The groupies, also known as the females flocking around KJ and his boys, look like straight video skanks. They're always willing to take whatever them dudes throw their way just to hang out with the crew. Those types of females are my worst enemies. But, like Mama told me when I first started having problems with KJ, every woman has her female foes. And, speak of the devils, there go Trecee and Misty, joining the pack.

~ 10 ~
Sistah Drama

*"Is this some kind of women's intuition
Some kind of insecurity?"*

—JILL SCOTT

"Oh no, them heffas ain't staring you down, Jayd," Mickey says, reacting to Misty and Trecee's obvious hatin' from across the food court.

"Jayd, we were going to wait to show you this on the way home, but we better show you now, just in case." Nellie reaches into her purse and hands me a balled-up letter.

"What's this?" I ask, unfolding the crumpled paper. It must have been read and then reread several times.

"It was going around school while you were in solitary confinement," Mickey says.

"I wasn't in solitary confinement and y'all still didn't answer my question," I say, looking from Mickey to Nellie and then from Misty to Trecee. They're pointing at me and rolling their eyes. Of course, they're talking about me.

"Just read the damn letter, Jayd," Nellie demands.

I open the letter and read it quietly to myself.

Misty,

> *What's up, girl? You were right all along. That bitch Jayd wants my man and I ain't having it. If Jason hadn't stopped me yesterday, I would have kicked her ass right then and there. But I'm glad we didn't fight yesterday*

'cause I had on my new sweat suit. I'm gone beat her down on Friday at lunch though. You down? I know you can't stand her ass either, so if you want to get a few blows in, be my guest. I can't wait to see her butt squirming on the ground, begging me to stop kicking her. She'll be sorry she ever tried to take my man from me.

Anyways, this class is so damn boring. What the hell I need to learn more English for? You my only real home girl at this punk ass school, know what I'm sayin? Meet me after school in the Main Hall so we can catch a ride with Jason to the mall. My man is suppose to be heading up there after practice and I want to make sure no hos get all up on him.

Trecee
—luvs—
KJ
4—Eva ✳

"What did Misty tell her?" I ask, folding the letter back up and handing it to Nellie, who unfolds it and reads it again.

"I don't know," Nellie says. "But whatever it was, she sure didn't paint her a pretty picture of you."

"I should go over there and sock her in the head for being stupid enough to listen to Misty in the first place," Mickey says, glaring hard at Trecee, who's now sitting on KJ's lap, staking her claim for all to see. Misty's standing over them, looking like Don King at a fight: hungry for a knockout punch.

"I want to slap Misty for being such a little instigator," I say.

"Don't let them get to you," Nellie says, trying to calm me down.

"It's all a mind game, Jayd. You know broads are better at

playing games than dudes," Mickey says, finally getting up to go get her candy.

"Mickey's right, Jayd. Those broads are just hatin' on you because you're pretty, smart, and you had KJ. Don't trip off them," Nellie says.

"She ain't gone do nothing on Friday, watch," Mickey says.

While taking a bite of my cheese on a stick, I look over at KJ and Trecee again and I start to feel real hot, like I'm going to burst into flames just like I do before I have a déjà vu vision.

"Is it hot in here or is it just me?" I say, fanning myself with a napkin.

"Maybe KJ got you all flushed inside," Nellie laughs.

"You're so silly, Nellie. KJ can't make me do all that," I say, sneaking another look at him. "Well, maybe not, but something is. You're sweating," Nellie says, passing me a napkin to pat myself down with.

Just as Mickey gets up to throw away her trash, I notice this White dude in the distance standing in line at Mrs. Field's. It's Jeremy's fine ass. God, he's a perfect distraction from the KJ drama.

"I'll be right back. I'm going to holla at Jeremy for a minute," I say, while continuing to pat my face with the napkin. "How do I look?"

"Like a little chocolate girl about to dip her hand in some vanilla ice cream," Mickey jokes.

Confident, I take a step in Jeremy's direction, but when I see him flash his bright smile at me, I freeze. I turn away from Jeremy and notice Trecee again. I can't take my eyes from her and once more I'm burning up.

"Jayd, I thought you were going over to get you some Jeremy?" Nellie asks, not noticing my hesitation or my eyes on Trecee.

"Yeah, in a minute," I say, trying to collect myself. But I'm still hot and I can't stop staring at Trecee. She's sitting on KJ's lap, licking on an ice-cream cone Misty brought her. My focus is so intent I swear she's going to catch me looking at her and come over to start something. But, she doesn't even notice me. I'm so hot I start fanning myself with my hands.

"Jayd, what's wrong? You feeling hot again? Girl, you need some hormone pills or something," Nellie asks, sounding concerned.

"Nah girl, I'm cool. I just need some air," I say, finally looking away from Trecee.

"I'm going to go have some cookies with Jeremy," I say, regaining my courage and cooling down a little. What else did Mama put in that bathwater last night?

I turn toward Jeremy and see he's already next in line at Mrs. Field's. If I hurry we can stand in line together and maybe he'll treat me to a cookie. That would be kinda cute, sort of like a first date. As I walk toward Jeremy, I see it's my turn to feel someone's eyes on me. I look across the food court to find Trecee now staring me down all while smiling and licking her chocolate ice cream.

As if in slow motion, the perfectly round chocolate scoop breaks away from its cone, conveniently missing Trecee and landing on KJ's pants; first in my head, then for everyone else to see. "Shit!" KJ yells loud enough for everyone in the food court to hear. He jumps up out his seat, and Trecee along with the remaining ice cream hit the floor hard.

"Damn it, Trecee. You just messed up my brand-new gear. What the hell is wrong with you?" KJ asks, not even trying to help her get up off the floor. I know she's embarrassed.

"I'm sorry, KJ. I didn't mean to, baby. I'll make it up to you," Trecee says, as pleasantly and as dignified as she can from the floor. But KJ ain't in the mood. If it's one thing he can't stand it's not looking good. And a dirty outfit ain't nowhere near looking good.

"Make it up to me?" KJ laughs. "You got three bills, Trecee, huh? Cause that's how much this suit cost and that's the only way you can make it up to me," KJ says, pulling on his pants and grabbing some napkins from the dispenser on the table. He is pissed.

I look over to see if my girls caught the action. They're watching all right, just like everybody else up in here. I can't believe it.

"Trecee, go get me some wet paper towels from the bathroom, and hurry up," KJ demands. "You better hope it don't stain. Then all you have to do is pay my dry cleaning bill." As KJ continues to humiliate Trecee in front of anybody within earshot, Trecee scrambles to get up, but keeps slipping in the melting ice cream. KJ's crew is clowning her hard, making the scene even more embarrassing for her.

"Dang dude, she can't even get up off the floor. Where'd you find this ho at, KJ?" Dell asks, loud enough for everyone to hear.

"I don't know, but I'm sending her ass back, just as soon as she pays me for my gear," KJ says, pointing to the ice-cream stains on his pants. Misty tries to help Trecee up, but Trecee just pushes her away, not wanting any charity, I guess. She looks like she's about to cry. I momentarily feel sorry for her.

I glance over to see if my man Jeremy is still standing by Mrs. Field's but damn, he's gone. Now I have to wait to see him in class tomorrow.

"Jayd, my man just called," Mickey yells to me. "I got to go pick him up from work." Mickey's man is always having car problems. It's time to go anyway. I can't take too much more of Trecee's humiliation, even if she does have it out for me. Besides, something at the back of my mind is telling me I may have had something to do with the drama playing out before me. The sweating, the feeling hot—all that has never happened to me before. Somehow it feels connected to what just happened between KJ and Trecee, but it's not something I really want to think about now.

"All right, girl, let's roll," I say, picking up our trash and taking it to the automatic garbage can.

"These things scare me. I feel like it's a Venus flytrap and I'm a fly," I say, placing the tray inside of the machine's opening, watching it devour the tray and trash in one swoop.

"Girl, come on. I can't keep my man waiting for long. He'll think I'm with some dude," Mickey says, walking toward the escalator.

"Your man knows you well, then," Nellie says, taking a free shot at Mickey.

"Whatever, Nellie. Do you want a ride home or not?" Mickey asks her while I walk behind them, trying to ignore the madness across the courtyard. I hope KJ and Trecee are happy together because they sure do deserve each other.

As we go down the escalator, posing like movie stars, I see Chance at the Verizon booth. He's such a cutey. If he wasn't so skinny and solely into White girls, I'd consider dating him. But, I don't think I'm his type anyway. For the year I've known him, I've only seen him with White girls; the skankier the better.

"Hey, Chance," I say once we reach the bottom of the escalator.

"Jayd and her girls, what's up?" Chance says, being funny.

"We have our own names," Mickey says, looking at me evil. She really wants to go and she doesn't too much care for talking to my friends in Drama. She says it's bad for her reputation.

"You're right. I'm sorry. I forgot who I was talking to. Hello, Mickey. Hello, Nellie," he says, giving them each a bow like a perfect gentleman.

"What's up, Chance?" Nellie says, smiling at his silly self.

"Are you going to Byron's party on Saturday?" she asks, hoping to pump him for valuable info on all of the inside gossip: will there be any celebrities there, what's on the menu, what's everyone wearing.

"Uhhh, no. Not my scene," he says, patting his stomach and looking toward the door. Actually, my boys and I are having a little get-together right now, if you want to come. Jeremy's there," he says, looking at me with that sly smile of his.

"Why you telling me," I ask, hitting him in the arm. "Besides, I know you're lying. He was just here getting some cookies."

"Yeah. He had the munchies," Chance says, chuckling a little.

"I hate to break this up, but anyone coming with me better come on," Mickey says, and she's not playing. She's left Nellie hanging in a dressing room on more than one occasion.

"Well, I kinda want to see what's up with y'all, but we don't have a way home," Nellie says, securing our ride before committing.

"Don't worry about that. We'll get you home," Chance says, putting his arm around Nellie and pinching me in the side.

"Okay, but I have to be home by five. Mama will get real suspicious if I'm home too late on a school day," I say. I know Chance is dependable and will get me home in time. He's picked me up from work before, so I trust him.

"Cool. I'll see y'all later," Mickey says, bolting out the door toward the parking lot.

"All right, let's get going. I just needed a new headpiece for my cell," he says, picking up his bag and heading out the door with his arm still around Nellie's shoulders.

"Hey, what about me?" I say, playing the jealous role. He loves it when I show him extra attention.

"Oh, you know Big Daddy got enough loving for all the honeys," he says, switching to straight pimp mode.

"Look, White boy, don't get full of yourself," I say, wrapping his right arm around my shoulders. Damn, he always smells so good. Today he must be wearing Polo.

"Chance, when are you going to get a new car?" Nellie asks as we head outside, approaching his classic Chevy Nova. It's a sweet ride, but not as nice as Jeremy's, in my opinion.

"This here is a classic, candy apple red, 1970 Chevrolet Nova SS with a 350 cubic inch, 300hp V8 engine as standard equipment, baby. You can't buy this kind of love," Chance says, opening the passenger door for Nellie to climb into the backseat.

"Now, you hear that, Jayd?" Nellie says, pulling the seat back so I can sit down in the front. "He just equated this hunk of metal with an emotion."

"Who you calling a hunk of metal?" Chance says, closing the passenger door before walking around to the driver's side.

"It's not a who; it's a what," Nellie says as he slides into the black vinyl seats. When he starts the car, I get a rush from the gun of the engine. They sure don't make them like this anymore, as Daddy would say.

"Like that, huh?" Chance asks, eyeing me like I just had an orgasm or something. But, I can't front; I do like it, a lot. I can't help wondering how Jeremy's car feels.

"Are you sure Jeremy's there?" I ask. "If he's not, I'm going to be very disappointed."

"Yeah, as a matter of fact, Matt just called me and I heard Jeremy in the background. He must've just got there," he says as we leave the parking lot, heading toward the beach. It's a beautiful afternoon in Redondo Beach. I can see the ocean so clearly from here.

"Can you turn your music down a little, please? The bass

is really giving me a headache," Nellie says, plugging her ears with her index fingers.

"Hell no. This is Outkast, baby. I can't help but bump this. Ain't that right, Jayd?" he says, smiling through his sunshades.

"It's not that bad, Nellie. Bryan always has his music up loud whenever he takes me anywhere," I say.

"Yes, but I'm usually not in the car with y'all, now am I?" she says. She can be a real tight-ass sometimes.

"We're almost there, so just sit back and enjoy the view, dude," Chance says, trying to mellow Nellie out.

"Where are we going, anyway?" I ask, realizing I have no idea where this so-called get-together is.

"We're going to Matt's house. It's right off of 190th, in the hills." As we make a right on 190th, Nellie starts to get suspicious of what kind of get-together we're going to.

"Are these your pothead friends, Chance?" Nellie asks, putting her arms on the back of our seats and placing her head in between ours.

"Yes, they are," Chance answers. That's one thing about these White boys out here; they love to smoke weed.

"Oh no," Nellie says, shaking her head and waving her hands dramatically, "I can't be seen hanging around pot-heads, Jayd. And, I don't want you tarnishing your good girl reputation either. Take us home now, please," Nellie says, sitting back in her seat like she's Ms. Daisy.

"Well, actually, it doesn't bother me so much, Nellie," I say, reminding her that I can speak for myself. "They've never pressured me to do anything I don't want to. Besides, my uncles smoke, my mom and her friends smoke, and the entire Drama Club smokes. So, I really think your reputation won't be tarnished if you're around it and don't partake," I say. I personally don't support the use of anything as a drug. But, I say, to each her own. Nellie's not convinced, but does agree to go along.

* * *

When we pull up to Matt's house, everyone's standing outside, admiring their cars and the girls up against them. And there it is: the classic Mustang sitting in the driveway with its owner nowhere to be found.

"What are these White girls hangin' all over the cars for?" Nellie asks, echoing my thoughts exactly.

"Girls like hot rods," Chance says, parking his car right behind Jeremy's.

"No, they don't. They like the money that belongs to the guys in them," Matt says, opening the passenger door to let us out.

"Hey, Matt," I say, giving him a big hug. We've grown cool through the Drama Club, as well. Out of all the cliques, I like this one the best. They're kind of the outcast floaters, like myself, but unlike Nellie. I can already see her getting a serious attitude when she sees the cigarette in Matt's hand.

"What the hell is this?" she says to Matt as he helps her out of the backseat.

"What, this?" Matt says, referring to the lawn party going on at his mansion. "This is Back to School Night, our way. I'm glad you two could join us. Adds a little color to the mix, know what I mean," Matt says, nudging me in the side with his elbow. Now, when White people say stuff like that, especially to my face, I want to go off. But, I know he doesn't mean anything by it and he doesn't know any better, so I'm going to let this one slide.

"Whatever, Matt," I say, following Matt and Nellie up the steep hill leading to the house. It's literally a mansion right on the beach. It's gorgeous in the inside. I know because Matt usually hosts all of the Drama Club's parties: another good reason to be affiliated with this clique. They give the best parties all year long, even better than the athletes and cheerleaders.

As we pass the couples and others sprawled out on the lawn, I don't see Jeremy anywhere. I hope I can make it to the bathroom before I see him. I want to check my makeup in the mirror and I have to pee.

"Hey, Matt. Where's the keg?" this blonde girl, Shelley, asks. She's wearing the slinkiest black bikini I've ever seen. And, she's as skinny as Paris Hilton. Why do dudes like these girls?

"It's by the pool," he says, gesturing toward the back of the house.

"Hey, why you didn't wait for me?" Chance asks as he grabs me around my waist, almost pulling me down the hill.

"Chance, be careful. I'm precious cargo," I say, squirming out of his embrace. "Where'd you go, anyway?"

"I went to tell your boy you're here. Come on. He's in the basement," he says, grabbing my arm and leading me into the house.

"Hey, where are you taking Beyonce?" Matt says, amusing only himself.

"I'm taking her to the basement. You coming, Nellie?" Chance says, reaching for her hand.

"Well, you're not leaving me with this fool. What's in the basement?" Nellie asks.

"You'll see," Chance says. With Matt following behind, we walk through the foyer laced with expensive art and a beautiful chandelier hanging from the ceiling. As we pass the large salt water aquarium to the right of the entrance hall, we enter into the kitchen.

Every time I walk into this kitchen, I can see Mama working her magic in here. It's been featured on HGTV more than once for its magnificent marble countertops. The cabinets are a beautiful maple wood with brass fixtures. There are two sinks: one strictly for cutting vegetables, which is in the center of the island, and the other for dishes. The stove is an antique, just like all the cars these rich kids drive. Only a few have sold out and bought BMWs and Benzs.

Chance leads us to the back of the room, through a door, and down a flight of stairs. The first thing that hits us is a cloud of smoke. The lights are dim and the music is mellow reggae; Burning Spear, I think. When we reach the bottom of the stairs, all I can see is glimmers of shiny cars and people sitting in big cozy chairs all around them. It's a garage for Matt's dad that doubles, apparently, as an entertainment room. There's a pool table in the back of the room and I can hear balls clinking up against one another. Everybody's just laid back; this is how the ballers roll.

~ 11 ~
Cookies and Cheddar

"Real guys go for real, down to Mars girls."

—OUTKAST

"Jayd, is that a Mercedes Benz, SL 500 over there?" Nellie asks, pointing to one of three cars lined up against the wall.

"Yes, I believe it is. And, that there is a CL 600, my dream car," I say. These dudes ain't playing when it comes to money. If the cars alone tell their families' income, they must be balling out of control. There are ten cars that I can count in the dim light and the basement must be the size of the entire house. I don't know what Matt's dad does, but he's rarely ever home. And, his mom is always home, but never around. Being the only child in this house must be heaven.

"Matt, can I use your bathroom?" I ask, trying not to inhale the smoke or scratch up the cars. Nellie's looking around in awe.

"Sure thing." Matt leads me through the crowded room to the back where there's a separate office area with a bathroom inside. When I turn on the lights, I see this is no ordinary bathroom.

"Damn," Nellie says, following me into the black and silver marble bathroom. "This is the baddest bathroom I've ever been in."

"It's just a place to crap. Enjoy," Matt says, turning around and closing the door behind him.

"Jayd, do you see this?" Nellie says, playing with the automatic brass faucet.

"Nellie, you act like you ain't never been nowhere before," I say, looking for my MAC Lipglass. I haven't seen Jeremy yet, but when I do, I want to be as cute as possible.

"Hold my backpack while I freshen up," I say, handing my heavy Jansport to Nellie.

"Jayd, what do you have in this bag, girl? KJ's ego?" she jokes, practically dropping the bag on her foot.

"That was a good one, Nellie," I laugh while carefully applying my Chestnut liner before coating my lips with gloss. "Be careful. My purse and charm bag are in there."

"It feels like you got the whole damn winter Coach collection in here. How the hell you suppose to look cute with his thing on your back?" She's got a good point. But, I don't have anywhere else to leave my bag while I socialize.

"Where's your backpack?" I ask, noticing for the first time that she only has her purse.

"I left it in my locker," Nellie says, totally unconcerned.

"How are you going to do your homework?" I ask, stunned at my girl's lack of interest in her education. She cracks me up sometimes.

"What homework? Girl, it's Back to School Night and the first week of school. You got homework in your classes?" she asks while taking my lip gloss from my hand and applying some to her bottom lip.

"Yes, I have quite a bit of homework," I say, slightly resentful at the huge difference between A.P. and General Ed. courses. There's got to be a happy medium between the two.

"Hey, do you think his dad is a lawyer? Who else could

bling like this?" Nellie asks while checking herself out one last time.

"I don't know. But, whatever he is, he ain't hurting for nothing," I say, momentarily envying Matt's life. Why couldn't I have been born with rich parents?

"Well, my family ain't hurting either, but we ain't rolling like this. This, Jayd, is OG." Nellie opens the bathroom door to return to the gathering, but I stay behind to finish up my business.

"I'll be right there. I still have to pee," I say, closing the door behind her.

"Hurry up. I don't know any of these people," Nellie says.

"Well, just wait a minute and we can walk in together," I say through the door.

"What's up?" I hear a male voice say to Nellie. "Talking to yourself?" he asks.

"My girl's in the bathroom. I don't think we've met. I'm Nellie."

"Hey, I'm Jeremy." And, there he was, my future baby daddy, outside chatting with my girl while I'm squatting on the fanciest toilet ever.

"Well, I've certainly heard a lot about you," Nellie says, about to blow my cover. Just then, I flush the toilet to shut her ass up. I wash and dry my hands on the pretty silver towels hanging from the beautiful brass towel rack. Mama would have a heart attack if we used the good towels to wipe our hands. Those towels are for guests only. And, here I'm the guest.

"Hey, Jeremy," I say, rushing out of the bathroom.

"Hey, Jayd. I heard you were here. How's it going?" he asks while squeezing past me to get to the bathroom, almost brushing his chest up against mine. Damn, he smells good.

"Excuse me," he says, smiling down at me.

"You're excused," I say, returning his smile and wishing I could just hug him up right now.

"I'll see you in the other room," I say, not wanting to leave. But, the boy has his own business to handle.

When Nellie and I return to the main room, the lights are on and the door leading to the backyard is open. People are hanging out by the pool and going in and out of the pool house. How big is this place? Nellie and I take a seat on the couch opposite the door, next to my Benz.

"Hey, girls. Can I offer you a drink?" Matt says, gesturing toward the wet bar on the other side of the room.

"No, I don't drink," I say, feeling a little awkward.

"You don't drink water, Coke, Dr. Pepper, or juice either?" he says, trying to be funny. "We also have hot tea, coffee, and a cappuccino maker. Just let me know and I'll get it for you," he says, turning toward Nellie.

"And, how about you?"

"I'll have a Vodka Cosmopolitan up, please," Nellie says, like she's on *Sex and the City*.

"You got it," Matt says, slightly amused by Nellie's ghetto boujie attitude.

When Matt leaves, I call her on her order. "Nellie, you don't drink," I say, pinching her in the arm.

"I know that. But I don't want to stick out like a sore thumb, like you do," she says, pinching me back. "Besides, I've always wanted to order a martini." And she's right. I'm the only one here that's not drinking or smoking something. I'm inclined to take a hit of someone's Newport, but I don't want to start that filthy habit. Almost everyone I know smokes, except for Mama. She says she can remember picking tobacco as a little girl back in New Orleans and would be damned if she's gone give them one cent of her money after all that labor she basically did for free.

"Are you ladies enjoying yourselves?" Jeremy asks, taking

us both by surprise. "Matt said this belongs to you," he says, handing Nellie her drink.

"Yes, I am. Y'all White boys sure know how to throw a party," Nellie says, looking around for any available boys to flirt with.

"I love coming over here, but I've never been in the basement before," I say, publicly acknowledging that I'm not a full-fledged part of this clique either.

"Yeah, this house is phat," Nellie says, still scoping the scene. "I think I'm going to take a walk outside," she says, suddenly becoming bold. She gets up and leaves me alone with Jeremy.

"I'm glad you decided to come down here and kick it with us. We're not so bad, are we?" he asks, taking a sip of his Guiness.

"Well, I don't know about all that. But, I'm glad I came too," I say, scooting over so he can sit down next to me.

"How do you like the cars?" he asks, spreading his legs to make himself more comfortable on the tiny couch. He's got to be at least 6 feet 4 inches.

"They're nice," I say. My grandfather would be in heaven.

"I saw you at the mall today," he says. "I tried to walk over to where you were, but there was some sort of commotion, and I needed to get back here, so I'm sorry I didn't say anything," he says, like he just lost my favorite pen. Why is he apologizing to me? I didn't even think he saw me, or would have gone out of his way to speak, for that matter.

"I saw you too. But, I don't think you owe me an apology for not speaking."

"Yes, I do. We're friends now, right? It's rude not to speak to your friends," he says, putting his beer down on the table next to the couch.

"Oh, so we're friends now, right?" I say, challenging his intentions. This White boy thinks he got game. He doesn't know I'm being schooled right now by KJ. I can top any game he brings.

"Yeah, we're friends. Everybody here is friends in some way," he says, looking past me and out the door, toward Nellie.

"Well, I can see you've made yourselves comfortable," Nellie says, coming back in from the pool with the same amount of drink in her glass she had when she left the room.

"Nellie, why don't you just put that down. You haven't touched it since Jeremy gave it to you," I say.

"Jayd, like I told you before, it's the look that matters, baby, the look," she says, bringing the glass to her face and pretending to take a sip. She's so silly; that's why she's my girl.

"So, guess what I just heard from Mickey?" Nellie says, like an international spy committing espionage.

"She called. What did you hear?" I say, teasingly.

"I heard that Trecee's only sleeping with KJ because he had a better car than the dude that she just broke up with over the summer," she says, tapping on my legs like she always does when she gets excited.

"KJ's car ain't all that. Her old Negro must've had a Pinto," I say, laughing at how girls can be so ridiculous sometimes. The girls in my hood rate guys according to three things: their gear, their hair, and their ride. That's how they decipher a dude's character: by how much cheddar he has.

"Well, ever since he tweeked his ride out last year, girls have been dropping the cookies in his lap like he's the cookie monster," Nellie says, putting her fist out for dap, for which I leave her hanging.

"Nellie, all girls don't care about material things," I say, refusing to put myself anywhere near Trecee's category. I'm nothing like that girl.

"But, you got to admit," Nellie says, focusing her energy

toward Jeremy, "girls like the cars with the booming systems, right Jeremy?"

"Yeah, I think girls like dudes with nice rides. But, it's up to the girl not to equate herself with the car," he says. I'm surprised by his comment. For some reason, I didn't expect him to be as smart as he seems.

"Well, Jeremy. It sounds like you have a little experience in this department," I say. "So tell me then, why is it that dudes are never satisfied with one girl? It's like they get these cars or tweek out the ones they already have to attract as many girls as possible. What's that about?" I ask, just knowing he can't answer my question.

"Well, it's all a game," he says, reaching for his beer. "Dudes at this age just want to have sex. Period. And, if you can do it while playing with a fine toy such as a car, why not?" he says, taking a huge gulp of his beer.

"Are you joking?" Nellie says. I know better than to take him seriously. I've already got Jeremy pegged as an instigator. He likes to have his fun.

"No, I'm not. Think about it; how many guys do you know with shitty cars who still have girls jocking them?" He's got a good point. If it weren't for KJ, Del, and C Money wouldn't get any play and they'd be at the bus stop with me.

"That doesn't make it acceptable," I say, ready for a good challenge. "You sound as if you're advocating the use of a vehicle to lure girls into bed."

"Not at all. I'm just saying girls like dudes with nice cars and guys like to have sex. It's an even exchange," Jeremy says with a very cunning smile on his face. This boy thinks he's got me right where he wants me.

"So, you wouldn't be hurt if a girl left you for a guy with a better car?" I retort.

"Not at all. But, finding a dude with a better car than me

would mean that I know the dude because he would be me," he says, proud of his wit.

"What the hell does that mean?" Nellie says, lost in translation. I think she must've got a contact high when she went to the pool house. I'm sure they're smoking up a storm in there. I'll stick with the secondhand cigarette smoke in here. That way Mama won't be suspicious when I come home. Cigarette smoke is as common as homeless people at the bus stop.

"That means he thinks his car is the hottest shit around," I say, giving her my quick version of his cocky words. "And, I agree; your car is nice. But the driver of any of these cars in this room would have a better chance at getting my cookies before you," I say, really kicking my flirting up a notch.

"Is that right?" he asks, readjusting his position to face me directly. "Funny, you never struck me as the type to exchange her cookies for cheddar," he says, looking me up and down, slowly waiting for my comeback.

"Well, you're right. But that doesn't mean that a guy can step to me with anything less than what I'm offering, understand?" I say, returning his strong gaze. I love his confidence. Just as Jeremy's gaze turns more flirtatious than challenging, Chance walks over, messing up the whole vibe.

"J man, they're waiting for you in the pool house. Reg and them brought the six-footer dude. Kristy and Leslie are taking turns and it's funny as hell. You gotta go see, dude," Chance says, pulling Jeremy up by the arm and exchanging places with him on the couch next to me.

"It'll have to wait, dude. We're in the middle of a very stimulating conversation," Jeremy says, trying to pull Chance back up.

"Nah, man. I've had enough. I need to sit down for a minute. The room is spinning," he says, putting his head on my shoulder.

"That's what you get for partaking in illegal behavior," Nellie says, in her original self-righteous tone. "It's not natural for your head to spin unless you have a fever. Do you have a fever?" Nellie asks, putting her hand up against Chance's head.

"Get your hands off me, girl," he says, playfully shooing Nellie back into her seat.

"All right. I'll be right back," Jeremy says, walking out the door toward the pool house.

"So, what'd I miss?" Chance asks, stretching his legs out across the couch, comfortably positioning himself across my lap.

"Well, just make yourself at home, why don't you?" I say, smacking him in the forehead. He's lucky he's my boy. Otherwise, his ass would be on the floor by now.

"I know Jeremy would like to make himself at home right here," he says, bracing himself for my impending blow.

"Boy, shut up," I say, smiling because I'm glad he thinks so. If it's one thing I've learned from living in a house full of men, it's that dudes talk as much as we do.

"What did he say about my girl?" Nellie's always asking the important question.

"He thinks you're fly, like everybody with good taste," he says, making me blush. These White boys know how to make a girl feel good, even if I'm just a friend.

"Really? How did he say it?" Nellie pries, unsatisfied with his simple answer. It was enough for me because I feel the same way about Jeremy.

"He just said it," Chance says, repositioning his head on my lap. "So, for real, y'all seemed in deep conversation when I walked up, or were you just playing Truth or Dare? If so, I pick Dare. Truth always gets me in trouble."

"No, fool," I say, pulling the bottom of my shirt from

under his head. "You need to get up. You're getting hair gel all over my shirt."

"You're going to have to get used to this. I think Jeremy uses the same kind," he says, rubbing his head on my shirt and jeans.

"Chance, you're a punk, you know that?" I say while pushing him and his sticky hair to the floor.

"I like this girl; she's got spunk," Jeremy says, walking back in from the pool house, obviously stoned. When KJ and his boys get high, they say stupid stuff too. That's why, unlike Nellie, I'm cool being the designated sober person: My mouth already gets me into enough trouble as it is.

"That was quick," Chance says, dusting himself off and taking a seat in the chair next to Nellie.

"Yeah, that was kinda short," Nellie says.

"How would you know? You've probably never even seen a bong, let alone know how long it takes to use one," I say, once again blowing her cover.

"Why you all up in my business?" Nellie says, sounding a little embarrassed. I didn't mean to put my girl on the spot, but sometimes she fronts a little too much.

"So, how was it?" I ask, redirecting my attention to Jeremy.

"It was what it was," he says with a big, goofy ass smile on his face. I notice that he never really answers a question. Instead, he gives incomplete answers that really annoy me. But, I guess I'll have to get used to that too, I smile to myself.

"Anyway, back to the subject at hand," Nellie says, getting us all back on track. "I believe the topic of debate was cookies for cheddar: Is it really an even trade?" Nellie says, sounding like Barbara Walters. "I think it was your turn, Jeremy. Can a sistah's milkshake be bought with dough?" she asks, using her martini glass as a microphone.

"Why are money and sex always equated to food?" I ask, annoying the hell out of Nellie.

"That is so not the point here. Stay on track, Ms. Jackson," she says, again pointing the glass at Jeremy. But, Chance beats him to the mic.

"Hell yes, it's even," he says, while Jeremy finally reclaims his seat next to me. Just the fact that he's in the same room with me gives me chills. Now that he's sitting next to me again, I feel an entire cold front coming on. "Okay look, I don't know about where y'all are from, but where I'm from, the bigger the chain, the more girls you catch," Chance says, showing off the diamond and platinum chain around his neck. Even the Notorious B.I.G. would be envious of his bling. That's the thing about rich White boys into hip-hop: They have the money to mimic their idols to the tee; pimp, players, and all.

"Dude, now you know it takes a lot more to get a girl than that overpriced piece of metal hanging around your neck," Jeremy disagrees. "Like I said earlier, women need to respect their value. If the woman equates what she thinks she's got to give with material shit, then that's her bad," Jeremy says, looking at me with blood-red eyes. He can't be that high: Nobody can be this insightful while intoxicated.

"I agree. Can a sistah get dinner first?" Nellie says.

"Maybe, if she's nice," Chance says, flirting with Nellie.

"Oh no, White boy. I need a man with a much better car than that old thing you drive," she says, shooting down his advance. Nellie would be caught dead first before she's seen with someone in a car like Chance's. Even if he's balling, he's still got to show it through his ride so that our neighborhood sees it. And, that means he needs to roll a Chrysler or an Expedition at the least. Not a Nova, no matter how classic it is.

"Damn, girl, do you see this bling around my neck? Do you know I had this handmade in Italy and the diamonds shipped from Africa herself?" he says, putting his chain directly in Nellie's face.

"I don't give a damn if your daddy owns the diamond mine," she says, getting up in his face to make her point completely clear. "It's the looks, baby. If you pick me up in that old-ass car, people are going to think you're a mechanic or something. And that's not enough for me."

"Well, what's the price? Maybe we can make an even trade," Chance says, playing with his chain and Nellie at the same time.

"See, that's the type of thing I'm talking about," I say, getting frustrated with their behavior. "She can't be bought, Chance. Besides, what good is that chain going to do her?" I ask.

"Yeah, do I get a matching one?" Nellie asks, enjoying the game with Chance.

"It's not funny," I say, trying to get my girl back on my side. I think she's been blinded by the ice hanging from his neck.

"Why are you getting so upset, Jayd?" Chance asks, backing up from Nellie and turning his attention toward me. "If two consenting young adults want to make a fair exchange, what's the problem?" he asks, sounding less high and more serious.

"The problem is multifaceted. First of all, you can't equate my cookies with that chain. Ever. That chain can't push a baby out of it, now can it?" I say, vexed that we're even having this conversation.

"Uh-oh. Here's the Jayd I know and love," Chance says, getting excited, like he's about to witness a good fight, which may not be far from the truth in a couple of days. "You should see her in action when she's really pissed," he says, hitting Jeremy on the leg.

"You know what, forget it. I can see my energy is being wasted on y'all anyway, including you, Nellie," I say, playfully kicking Nellie's Candies boots.

"That's why I don't engage in too many debates: It's futile," Jeremy says, again adding his enlightened two cents. "People are going to do what they want anyway, car or no car, bling or no bling," he says, pulling his baseball hat low onto his face, sinking down into the couch and closing his eyes.

"My boy J here is right," Chance says, leaning back in the oversized leather chair, identical to Nellie's, revealing his flawless custom-made Tims. "If the girl wants to give it up, it's all on her. What are we going to do, say no?" he adds.

"That's not exactly what I said, but close enough," Jeremy says, giving Chance a slight nod.

"I think you're both wrong," I interject, ready to kill this sexist conversation. "Yes, it's a sistah's responsibility to value her body; I totally agree. But, the dude has some responsibility too. He has to respect and value his body as well as the girl's. Why is it always on the girl? And, why are men so obsessed with sex and money?" I say, really wishing I could ask KJ that question. It's not like I'd expect an honest answer from him, but still: I should've asked.

"Okay, y'all are bringing me down," Jeremy says, sitting straight up and bending over, placing his elbows on his knees. "We're both wrong. We're both screwed up for even referring to sex the way we do. Jayd made a good point earlier that wasn't addressed: Why do we equate these things with food?" he asks, displaying his good listening skills. He's capable of holding an intelligent conversation and he's a good listener. Can the boy be any more fly?

"When I was little, my auntie Ron use to give me oatmeal cookies and cheddar cheese as a snack. I never thought it would one day be a substitute for sex and money. That said, I think it's because they're both necessities, like bread and butter," I say. "Both girls and guys need to act differently if we want different results," I say, supporting my soon-to-be man.

"Well said," Jeremy says, giving me a nod in agreement.

"No, not well said. That statement assumes that dudes want different results, and we don't, or at least I don't. I'm very satisfied with having my sweet ass ride and honeys coming in and out, know what I'm saying, J?" Chance says, raising his hand to Jeremy's for a high five.

"I'm going to have to leave you hanging on that one, man. I don't like a bunch of different girls in my ride. Too much drama," he says, smiling at me. What does he know about drama?

"This looks like a party for the Debate Club, not the thespians," Matt says, interrupting our private vibe.

"Hey, Matt, this is some shit right here. These girls are something else," Chance says, shaking his head like he's been defeated.

"I believe it," he says, looking more stoned than Jeremy and Chance combined. "Oh, yeah. The first sober shuttle is here, if you ladies have somewhere to be," he says, leaning onto Nellie's chair for support.

"What the hell is that?" Nellie asks, still holding her full drink.

"It's our designated driver shuttle. We always have one with our parties. We like to live wild, but still live, know what I mean?" Matt says, putting a smile on Nellie's face.

"These cats have style," Nellie says, holding her glass up in salute.

"Was there something wrong with the drink?" Matt asks, noticing she hasn't touched it. "I can have the bartender make you another one before you go."

"She doesn't drink," I say, completely busting her cover. Nellie's face falls and she gives me the evil eye. "Come on, Nellie. It's time for us to roll," I say, not wanting to leave, but knowing that it's way past my play time. I feel like the streetlights are on and Mama's standing on the porch, waiting for me to come inside.

"Leaving so soon?" Jeremy asks, gently grabbing my hand. "I was looking forward to talking some more. I promise I'll go easy on you this time," he says, revealing his perfect smile.

"Funny, I thought I was too hard on you," I say, releasing his hand and getting up, grabbing my backpack on the way.

"Wow, did you feel that?" Chance says, looking around the room. "Was that an earthquake, or did y'all just create some serious seismic energy up in here?"

"Good-bye, stupid," I say, socking Chance in the shoulder.

"Why the abuse? I'm on your side," he pleads, pretending to be hurt. "You don't have to be so hard on me too," he says, like a wounded puppy.

"We'll see y'all at school tomorrow," I say, following Nellie back up the stairs toward the kitchen.

"It was a pleasure, boys," Nellie says, giving a Hollywood wave from the top of the stairs.

"Believe me, the pleasure was all ours," Jeremy says, looking right at me. I turn back around and walk up the stairs, speechless for what must be the first time in my life. This boy is something else.

When we get outside, the same girls and guys are hanging around, plus about twenty or so new faces. The sober shuttle is actually the school's Drama Club van. I'm sure they worked it out that this party somehow fits into official club business. I'm just glad they have the good sense to have a sober van, even if the designated driver, Seth, has questionable mental stability without being under the influence of anything.

"Hey, En Vogue. Aren't you short a member?" he says, acknowledging Mickey's absence.

"Just shut up and drive," Nellie says, already irritated with him. She has little patience for people she don't know making small talk with her.

"Hey, Seth. Please don't drive like a maniac and get us

back to Compton safely," I say, taking a seat right behind him, directly across from my girl. We're the only ones on the van. I guess everybody else at the party is just getting started.

"No problem, Lady J. One, nonstop direct ride to the CPT coming right up," he says, pushing the button, closing the automatic sliding door. As we pull out the driveway, heading back east toward home, I wonder if Jeremy misses me already, as I do him. After all this mess with Trecee and KJ blows over, maybe we can talk some more. I haven't been that attracted to someone and stimulated by their mind in a long time.

"Hey, girl, what you wearing to school tomorrow?" Nellie asks.

"I don't know. I was thinking about wearing my jean miniskirt and a big off-the-shoulder shirt. But, I'm not sure yet. Why?" I ask, not really caring. I'd rather daydream about Jeremy some more than snap back into the reality of having to face another day at Drama High tomorrow.

As we cruise down 190th, listening to Seth sing along with the Black Eyed Peas, the scenery quickly changes from big houses with lush lawns to a busy industrial area. There's really no direct way to get from this part of the South Bay to Compton. So, going down 190th until we're able to hit Artesia, which merges with the 91 freeway, is the best way to go. Mickey comes this way, too.

"Who gets dropped off first?" Seth asks in between songs.

"I do. Just drop me off at the bus stop on Alondra. I'll walk the rest of the way," I say.

"Jayd, why don't you let the boy take you all the way home?" Nellie says, putting her iPod down and looking at me. "It's getting late. You shouldn't be walking around by yourself anyway."

"I'll be fine. Besides, I don't want him knowing where I live," I say, playing with Seth. He's dropped me off after plays before, so he already knows my address. It's really Mama asking questions I'm worried about.

"Yeah, you never know what I might do," Seth says, playing along. "All right, Jayd, here you go. Be careful," he says, waving at me as I get out of the van, leaving Nellie in his care.

"Get my girl home safely, man," I say. "Text me when you get to the crib," I say to Nellie.

"All right, Jayd. And, don't wear that miniskirt yet. I'm going to wear mine next week and we can match," she says as they pull off. My girl, my girl. The truth is I don't have much choice. I only have a certain amount of stuff at Mama's. Everything else is at my mom's. I would wear the skirt on Friday, but I might be scrapping and I don't want all my goods showing. So, I'm saving my other pair of jeans for then.

"Hey, girl. Where you coming from?" Bryan says, sneaking up behind me. He must be coming from his part-time job at Miracle Market.

"I had a meeting," I say, knowing he ain't buying my lie. But, it's what I'm sticking with.

"If you say so. How's the KJ drama going?" he asks, pulling out a joint from his backpack, putting it behind his ear. As he slips his bag over his shoulder, his phone rings and he doesn't answer it.

"Dodging the honeys again, I see," I say, pulling his chain. "Why do guys have to be dogs?" I ask him, not really expecting him to answer.

"Girl, you don't know? Cookies can make a man crazy. And, vice versa for the girls and whatever they want from the man. It all makes us do some strange things, like dodging girls that call you every hour on the hour," he says, erasing the phone number from his inbox. He's right; this whole day was strange. And, this situation with KJ was even stranger. Maybe Bryan can give me some advice on how to handle KJ, and a little insight on Jeremy too.

~ 12 ~

Déjà vu and Other Strange Things

"Flee from hate, mischief and jealousy
Don't bury your thought, put your dreams to reality."

—BOB MARLEY

"The sooner you understand that men and women think differently, the better," Bryan says, putting his phone in his pocket, giving me his full attention. "I'm surprised you even asked the question, especially considering you're the only girl in a house full of dudes. I thought you'd know this by now," he says, sounding slightly disappointed.

"Just because I know it doesn't mean I understand, especially if it doesn't make any damned sense," I say, pushing him with my shoulder. Bryan's by far my favorite uncle.

"All right, what happened at school today?" he says, knowing I'm irritated about something.

"Nothing in particular. It's just KJ and his bull, you know, the usual," I say, dodging a pit bull coming my way. "Why don't people keep their dogs on leashes?"

"You know what, Jayd? You're asking some real stupid questions today," he says, laughing at me. "When's the last time you've seen a dog on a leash around here? You'll be lucky if they walk them with chains," he says, telling the truth.

"All right, that was a stupid question. But my first one wasn't. Why can't dudes understand that no amount of panties is worth this much drama?" I say, secretly wishing KJ could be more like Jeremy in personality. Jeremy doesn't give off player vibes at all.

"Because most boys KJ's age don't think that far ahead. They're all about the game, which is literally cat and mouse. Once the cat catches the mouse, there's nothing else he can do with it but play; it's the cat's nature."

"What the hell kind of analogy was that, Pepe le Pue?" I say, socking him in the arm.

"I'm just telling the truth. I don't want you to think too hard about this, Jayd, 'cause there's really not a lot of worrying going on on KJ's side, believe me. I've been in his situation a couple of times, and all the brother wants to do right now is retreat." Just then, I get a text from Nellie saying she made it home.

"Who's that? See, girls play games too," Bryan says, reaching for my cell.

"It's just Nellie, fool," I say, showing him her name on my screen.

"That doesn't mean anything. You know girls swing both ways more often than not," he says, running ahead of me up Gunlock, toward home. It's evening time on our block, which means the smell of beans and fried chicken permeates the air, making me hungry. I hope Mama's making something good tonight. What am I saying; she makes something good every time she cooks.

"Whatever, Bryan. Me and my girls don't roll like that," I say, not walking any faster. I'll catch up with him at the house.

"Not yet. But, that's beside the point," he says, slowing down, allowing me to catch up with him. "Men are better at games because they know how to tap into the emotional element. And, women are all emotional beings," he says, falling into stride with my step. "Once a man taps into that element, everything else is his," he says, cupping his hands like he's holding something precious in them.

"So, what you're saying is it's the woman's fault for falling victim to her emotions," I say, ready to attack his convoluted theory.

"No, Sistah Soulja. What I'm saying is women have to step up their game if they want the playing field to be equal.

"But, why does there have to be a playing field at all? Why can't we just be honest and satisfied with each other without all the BS?" I say, sounding naive.

"Because, the fun's in the chase. As strange as it sounds, it works. That's just the way it is, Jayd. If you're going to date in this lifetime, get used to having plenty of drama around you at all times," he says, pulling his shirt out of his pants and passing me his backpack as we approach home. "Speaking of which, tell Mama I'll be back later. I've got some business to handle," he says, passing the house up and walking down the street to only God knows where.

When I walk in the house, I see Mama's already in the kitchen, working her magic like only she can.

"Hi, Mama. Bryan said he'll be home later. How was your day?" I say, putting my backpack on the floor and Bryan's on the chair next to the dining room table before walking into the kitchen to give Mama a kiss and get to work.

"My day was fine, baby. How was yours?" she says while putting a big pot on the stove.

"It was okay. I went to the mall with Mickey and Nellie after school," I say leaving out the rest. I hate lying to Mama, so I'll just avoid the rest of the truth instead. I knew she didn't remember that I got out early today. That's one thing about Mama; she's not into the school's business. She's just glad that I go on a regular basis and get decent grades, just like my mom. Everything else is irrelevant.

"Mama, how come I always have so much drama around me when it comes to these girls? Trecee sent some stupid note to Misty talking about fighting me on Friday. And, I'm tired of this mess," I say, picking up the onion on the table, ready to slice it like it's KJ's head. "Why does this always happen to me?" Mama doesn't say anything for a long, long time. When she pauses like this, I know not to interrupt her thoughts. It's usually to let me think about what I just said before she adds her fifty cents. I start to peel the onion as Mama begins to speak.

"From the beginning," Mama said, "I knew you were different. You almost didn't make it, girl. I thought your stubborn behind would never pick the right year to be born. But, you had to come when you thought it was right, not when I wanted you to come."

Mama loves to tell stories while we're in the kitchen. I love to listen while I chop the onions, or grate the cheese, or sift the flour, or clean the greens—whatever she and Jay tell me to do. They're the masters of the kitchen. Her stories are always humorous, long, and full of half truths, which is what makes them the most interesting.

Every time she tells the story of my birth, I get a little nervous because I'm not so sure I want to hear it. It's starting to feel like déjà vu, and I think she can sense this. I also don't like hearing it because it always reminds me I wasn't planned.

My mom was pissed to discover she was pregnant right when she finally decided to leave my dad. I don't need to feel any worse right now. What do I need to hear this for? But, I do love to hear Mama talk. And it's rare for us to be alone in the evening. Everyone's usually home by now.

"Mama, what does this story have to do with Trecee wanting to fight me?" I ask, a little irritated. I really need Mama's advice right now, not some mystical story about how I was born.

"The story of your birth helps you to understand your place in the world. If you would remember it when you have these problems I wouldn't need to repeat it so much. Now, shut up and listen. This is also part of your homework: listening for your lesson. Hand me that wooden spoon over there."

I walk over to the overly crowded kitchen counter and grab the wooden spoon. I sit down, pull a paring knife out of the raggedy blue plastic dish rack and start cutting onions for the red beans and rice.

"You almost didn't make it," Mama continues. "Your mama and daddy had been married for only seven months, and they were breaking up already. Oh, those two could fight and make up. But, this time was different. Your mama couldn't take it anymore. She moved in with him to get away from home, so in her mind she couldn't come back here. So, she went and stayed with your aunt Vivica.

"Your aunt Vivica, her husband, and your mama all went to Vegas for a weekend getaway. Well, your daddy went down there to get away too. As the universe would have it, they ran right into each other for one more night in Vegas. That, my child, is when you decided to be conceived. In the middle of the desert, on a hot night in late June.

"You were born on your mama's birthday. She wasn't happy at all. Oh, I remember that. Your mama complained during the whole pregnancy. She said you took everything— her beauty, her energy, her waistline. But, more importantly, you took her birthday, which y'all now have to share."

I've always had these daydreams, or premonitions, if I can call them that. Anyways, right before something is about to happen, I have a déjà vu type experience, sometimes preceded by a hot flash, like the one I had in the mall earlier. Mama's the only person I can talk to about these things. She says it's because I was born with a caul on my head.

It was my mom's twentieth birthday. She was out celebrating with my aunts. Mama said my mom had just gotten her hair done, her shoes were new and her nails were fly. She was rocking a fresh new miniskirt with one of them big loose off-the-shoulder shirts that fit tight at the hips. At nine-months pregnant, my mom was looking hot. She said she wasn't let-tin' no baby get in the way of her celebrating her birthday.

They were all dancing and having a good time when my mom's water broke. She went into labor right there on the dance floor. I guess that's why I like music so much. Well, by the time we all got to the hospital I was on my way, and Mama was right there. It was just before midnight and the doctors were amazed at how easily I came into this world. Smooth as silk, because of the caul on my head, if you let Mama tell it.

A caul has superstitious tales associated with it that date way back past slavery to our time in West Africa. Mama says that where she grew up, cauls are respected for their powers and their uniqueness. Children born with cauls are seen as special because they have a direct link to their ancestors, which gives them the gift of sight. Children born with cauls are usually girls. These children also suffer during their child-hood because of their uniqueness and because they seem to always have drama happening all around them.

"You would have been a queen had we stayed in Nawlins, Jayd. You and your mom, because you're my daughters and your blood is strong. Understand that there will always be drama in your life. Always. As long as you're Jayd Jackson, granddaughter of mine. You just have to deal with it."

There are good caul stories and bad caul stories. Mama al-ways tells me both sides to everything. She also says the re-sponsibility of the caul is in the hands of the mother. The mother is supposed to take the caul, wrap it carefully in a clean piece of cheesecloth or another cotton garment, and bury it in the garden of the house the child will live in.

"If this ritual of reverence and respect is performed, the child and her powers will be protected always and she will have guidance from the ancestors. If this is not done, she won't have her rightful protection and guidance, and she'll have to learn her power by way of wisdom, which comes out of suffering and drama, in your case.

"Considering the circumstances of your birth, your mama wasn't trying to hear too much else, especially not about something wrapped around her baby's head. The doctor saw the thin, purplish-blue membrane covering your head and thought it was choking you. He took it and threw it in a pile of biologically hazardous waste to be burned. Your caul never received a proper burial.

"It was burned, my little fire child, and your destiny cannot fulfill itself in any other way. This is why, I suspect, your visions are limited to your dreams, unlike your mother and me." My grandmother pours the last of the tomatoes into the huge boiling pot of beans, and turns to me with a warm smile on her face.

"I cried for a month when they told me they burned it. Then one night when you were almost a month old, I had a dream of a child bursting out of a ball of flames that seemed it was big enough to fill all of eternity. This child emerged with some scars, but overall, she was healthy and stronger for it. I never feared for your survival after that.

"I knew that your path would be rough, yes, but impossible, never. Instead of the power of sight, you have the power of words. Like the charm bag I gave you. There are words written on them you need to pay close attention to. You'll learn of your special path and powers as time passes. Now, chile, it's time to make the corn bread."

Mama may have been trying to make me feel better and maybe even a little special by telling me about my path and powers, but the first time she told me this story I was scared. The first power I need to learn about is how to squash this mess with Trecee without getting into combat with her. I really need a way to make it through the rest of this week without any more bull from Misty, Trecee, or KJ.

"But, Mama, you ain't helped me figure out what to do," I say, passing her the sifted cornmeal. She starts to melt the butter in a cast-iron skillet while shaking a little of the cornmeal over the melting butter. It gives her corn bread a special crispy crust that melts in your mouth. Mama can throw down in the kitchen.

"Jayd, what do you want me to say? Sometimes you have to do things you don't want to do. In your case, you also have to be careful of wishing bad things on people." Mama picks up the bowl of corn bread batter and pours it into the skillet, which she puts in the oven to bake. The scent engulfs the entire kitchen, and so does the heat.

"It's hot in here. I need to get some air," I say, moving toward the back door. I can't deal with any more mystical homework or cleansings or anything. I've got to figure out how not to whip this girl's ass in two days.

"You're a fire child, Jayd. I've told you that many times, and yet you still don't hear the lesson in the story," Mama says. "You may regret the circumstances of your birth but you can choose how to react to the story of your birth, just like you can in this situation with Trecee." Mama stops talking to take a sip of her water. "Keep a cool head, listen, and be patient. You can control your powers like you can control your actions. Now go think about that for a while." Mama says, shooing me out the door.

I love my grandmother, but she can confuse a sistah at times. That's why I got my girls. They kept it real, especially Nellie. I'll have to speak with them again tomorrow about what to do. They don't always give the best advice, but at least I understand exactly what they're saying, when they say it. Now, it's time to think about my homework. I have three chapters to read for Government, and I ain't even thought about my other classes yet. Oh well, tomorrow will come whether I'm ready for it or not.

~ 13 ~
Fire Child

"Fire, fire, fire, burning fire
It's burnin' so high and they can't put it out."

—SIZZLA

My mouth has always been my biggest problem. If it isn't getting me into trouble at home, it's always getting me into some mess at school. I don't really talk about anyone behind their back, but rather I tell people what I feel to their face. They usually don't appreciate the directness of my ways, so I'm confused. Am I supposed to keep my opinions to myself, even if it just needs to be said? I don't think so.

"Are you going to talk to Trecee, or are we going with Mickey's plan?" Nellie asks.

"Jayd, you ain't gone get nowhere with that girl," Mickey says as we walk toward her locker. We're in the Main Hall and it's packed, as usual. It's five minutes before fourth period and I need to get to class. We're walking against the majority of the oncoming student traffic and people keep knocking into me.

"I don't know about fighting Trecee tomorrow, but if one more person bumps into me without saying 'excuse me,' I'm gone whip somebody's ass," I say. That's one thing about these White folks—they don't say excuse me when they bump into you. They can almost knock your butt down and never even look back.

"Then why don't you say something to one of them?"

Mickey suggests, teasing me. She knows I ain't gone say nothing. I'd say something, but I don't want any more negative vibes, know what I mean? "Whatever, Mickey," I say, rolling my eyes at her. She can be rude when she wants to be. Her little attitude is what gets her hated on by other broads. Like I said before, it's my mouth that gets me into a whole heap of mess.

Take for example this whole situation with Trecee. On Tuesday, she tried to jump me in front of my locker. On Wednesday, she sent a little note to Misty saying she's going to jump me on Friday. Well, it's Thursday now and I don't want to waste any more time. So I've decided to be the bigger person and step to her to squash this mess.

"I think you should just walk right up to her and knock her ass out. That's what I'd do," Mickey says while inspecting her extra-long, airbrushed, acrylic nails. She's obsessed with her looks. She gets her nails done every Friday, so I know she's bugging out by now because her polish has moved up from the cuticle just a tiny bit, indicating that her nails ain't fresh.

"Mickey, how the hell I'm just gone walk up to someone and sock them in the face? This ain't no beat-down," I say, knowing Mickey don't feel me. She's straight gangsta when she has to be. No warning. No talking. Just straight blows. As bougie as Nellie is, I don't know how she and Mickey ever became friends.

"Thanks for the sound advice, home girl, but I think I'll do this my way," I say. We get to Nellie's locker and wait for her while she gets her books out.

"And what way is that?" Nellie asks. "Avoiding her or just telling her off so tough that she can't say nothing back?"

Nellie, who hates arguing, always admires the way I can tell people off, especially girls. She's not good with confrontation.

"Nah. I'm just gone try reasoning with her," I say. I've given this a lot of thought, especially since my hot-flash episode yesterday and I don't want to hurt anyone if I don't have to. I don't want to be responsible for what happens to Trecee as a result of her stupidity and my impatience. I also don't want to get hurt myself. I just need to reason with her, if that's at all possible.

"Reasoning with her?" they ask in unison.

"Yes, reasoning, vibing, getting her to listen to me."

Nellie and Mickey both look dumbfounded.

"Why are y'all so shocked? Have people completely forgotten how to talk to one another?"

"Jayd, this ain't no damn meeting. This is a fight. A hair-pulling, lip-busting, shirt-ripping fight. You the only one who don't see that and that makes you stupid," Mickey says.

The bell rings for class and everyone is rushing through the halls. So far, no one else has bumped into me, but my guard is up and ready.

"I'll see y'all later. Thanks for the advice," I say sarcastically.

"Whatever, Jayd. You better get with the program or she gone catch you off guard," Mickey says while checking her text messages from her man.

"We're out. See you at lunch," Nellie says. Nellie and Mickey are off to fourth period and I'm left to plan my meeting with Trecee. In order to talk to Trecee, I'll have to wait until lunch and go over to South Central. I'll think of how to say what I want to say while in Government.

I walk away from Nellie's locker and turn back down the Main Hall toward class.

"Hey, Jayd. How's it going?" Jeremy asks, sneaking up behind me. "Did you do last night's reading?"

This boy's got me so nervous I can hardly speak. "Yeah, I managed to get through it. How about you?" I ask, amazed that I'm walking to class with one of the most sought-after boys on campus.

"It was boring. But I'm kinda used to Mrs. Peterson," he says with the biggest smile on his face. He's so cute. "She can be a real witch sometimes. If you get on her bad side, kinda like you did yesterday, she'll never forget it."

"I didn't mean to," I say, remembering yesterday's battle over the Constitution. "It's just that it gets under my skin how some teachers can ignore history."

"Hey, I feel you. Last year she actually doubted the Holocaust ever happened, and my great-grandmother's whole family was wiped out. Like I said, a witch." Jeremy opens the classroom door and follows me to our seats. As soon as we sit down, the late bell rings and Mrs. Peterson starts right in on me as if I'm the only person in this classroom full of students. I try to stay calm and not trip, but Mrs. Peterson is sweating me hard.

"Miss Jackson, what do you think of the U.S. Constitution? Is it a waste of paper, like you said yesterday?" I look at her with such intensity I think she'll burst into flames. Then I check myself, remembering yesterday's ice-cream incident.

"Or," she continues with a twisted grin, "would you like to retract your statement after doing last night's reading assignment on the amendments?"

My initial response is a resounding "hell no" but I don't want to go there and she isn't finished yet.

"Is it a waste of paper, and therefore trees, and therefore a waste of the very air we breathe, as you so eloquently stated yesterday, or not, Jayd?" Her dramatics are finished and now it's my turn.

Man, she's got a great memory, or else she writes down everything we say for later use. Either way, she's got me on this one, and because she's being so snide about it, I have to give her a run for her money.

"I didn't say it was a waste of paper," I say with all of the attitude meant for Trecee. "I said that paper and ink were both wasted on writing the Constitution because it states that slaves—Black people, in case you forgot—were said to be only three-fifths of a person for tax purposes, and they're otherwise referred to as property. This document demeans and offends the same citizens who are supposed to abide by these laws, the same document that's now supposed to protect them. The entire document is tainted. Because of these facts, I think the Constitution—in order to be effective and fair—needs to be rewritten so that none of the citizens mentioned in the Constitution feel degraded and instead feel valued and protected."

Everyone in the classroom starts clapping and whistling, including Jeremy, who looks very impressed. Mrs. Peterson, on the other hand, doesn't look impressed in the least. In fact, she looks upset.

"Are you down off your soapbox now, Miss Jackson?" She doesn't really give me a chance to respond; she doesn't even look my way. "Good. Well, Miss Jackson, I do understand how *you* might be upset. However, I don't think that one little portion of the entire document should be a cause to rewrite the entire Constitution. Moving on. . . ."

I can't help myself. She always has the last word, and this time, it's not happening. I raise my hand and respectfully, but with attitude, say, "Excuse me, but first of all, I don't think I'm the only person who should be upset.

"And by your exaggerated *you* I assume you meant because I'm Black, and I resent that. Everybody should be upset that we were even slaves, including you. And we all need to understand that it's not one little portion—it's a soiled document, plain and simple, and it has committed far more than one offense."

I thought she'd have a heart attack right then and there—just die on me. Flat out, on the floor, glasses and all. You see, Mrs. Peterson don't like me too much already and it's only the third day of school. She's already accused me of "insubordination"—one big word for saying I don't respect her, and she's right. Most of the teachers up here are just like her. They're White, upper-middle class, either overweight or underweight (in her case, over), and they don't tolerate different people. That's South Bay High.

Mrs. Peterson also has a thing about her "rules." She likes to run her class like Congress, where she's the House Speaker, and we're her little representatives. Well, I'm a "rebel with a mouth" as Mama would say, so she can't speak for me—I speak for myself. And I don't appreciate her making light of this issue. I'm already upset that Trecee is tripping off some stupid mess, now this.

"Miss Jackson," Mrs. Peterson says with her teeth clenched, her jaw tight and her gray-dyed-red hair standing straight on end. She's tapping her foot and her hip is moving up and down. She's so short and wide though, you can hardly see it. So far, I've learned Mrs. Peterson only taps her foot when she's talking about the Kennedys in Congress (she's a Republican) or when she's had enough of a student and is about to bring her wrath down upon them.

"Miss Jackson, you speak of things you know nothing about, and you also speak out of turn, rudely interrupting me." Just then, Mrs. Peterson does something Jeremy says she rarely does: She smiled at me. Because this was unexpected, I didn't know what to think. I just knew it couldn't be a good thing.

"You seem to have a profound interest in the Constitution, Jayd, so therefore, I'll allow you to handwrite the entire Constitution, highlighting all portions dealing with slavery, or so you think. You may go to the library and stay there until you're done."

No, she didn't. I can't believe her. She's so unpredictable. Now, what do I do? I guess to the library I go.

~ 14 ~
What to Do

"Everything you do or say
You got to live with it everyday."

—INDIA ARIE

Since I spent the rest of fourth period in the library, I was able to come up with a plan to talk to Trecee. If I can get her before she gets over to South Central, I may be able to talk to her without an audience. I need to find my girls first though and tell them about this crap with Mrs. Peterson and that Jeremy walked me to class.

When the bell rings, I walk out of the library, across the courtyard where the skaters hang, and over to the main lunch quad where South Central hang. There's Nellie and Mickey sitting on the benches that outline the quad; Trecee's nowhere in sight. Momentarily forgetting my search for Trecee, I sit down next to Nellie and join their animated conversation.

"I can't believe it's already Thursday. I have no idea what I'm going to wear to the back-to-school party at Byron's house on Saturday night. Isn't there also a fight party in the hood that same night?" Nellie says, slyly reminding me I'm supposed to be in training or something for my big fight tomorrow. I begin to protest, but Mickey cuts me off.

"You're going to the party, Jayd, and we won't take no for an answer." Mickey always likes us to go to parties together. She says we're protected from haters that way. But personally, I'm not much of a party girl, especially not the parties out here.

These White folks get crazy, drinking kegs and doing all kinds of drugs and stuff. If I didn't know Chance so well and know Matt from Drama Club, I would have agreed with Nellie's way of thinking yesterday. At the house parties in Compton, fools do drink forties and smoke weed, but that's it. Usually it ends with somebody shooting, but at least they ain't snorting coke and running trains on drunk girls.

All the dudes up here ain't like that though. Byron is this fine, White football player who has a thing for Nellie. She's "cute, dark, and lovely," as she likes to tell it, and very fashion conscious. Byron seems to like all there is about Nellie. So, as friends of Nellie's, we're all invited to the party that will determine who will be part of the most popular cliques for the rest of the year: the "All-Sports, Back-to-School House Party"—no parents allowed.

"Byron is so sweet to host this party. Girl, it's going to be off the chain! All the cute guys and girls are going to be there. We have got to look hella good for this party," Nellie says.

"Girl, you're right. We have to go to the Swap Meet after school, and get our nails done . . ." Mickey says, getting excited.

"The Swap Meet? Girl, no. Ain't nobody shopping at the Swap Meet for this party. We all have to go to the mall and get some fly gear from a real store, not a booth," Nellie says, insulted that Mickey would even suggest Swap Meet gear for such an important event.

"Nellie, you act like we got money or something. We may go to school with rich people, but we ain't rich. I'm with Mickey on this one," I say, looking in my backpack for some change to buy Doritos from the vending machine. Mickey's boyfriend gives her an allowance, so she can go around flash-

ing the fly Swap Meet gear, but not Mall gear. Nellie sometimes forgets our parents aren't as well off as hers.

"I'm going to get something from the machines. Y'all want
something?" I ask, getting up from the bench.

"We already got our snacks," Nellie says, showing me her
Gummi Bears. As I walk across the quad in my own world,
thinking about what I already have that can be worn to this
party and what I'm gone say to Trecee when she shows up, I
spot KJ coming out of the cafeteria with his crew. He looks
flawless, wearing a white and silver Enyce suit, with a flock of
chicks right behind him, though Trecee isn't among them.

I get my chips out of the machine and head back to the
benches where my girls are sitting. Still no sign of Trecee. By
the time I reach the bench, I feel someone following me. KJ
walks up behind me and touches me on the shoulder.

"What's up, Jayd? Can I sit down and catch up with you
and your girls? What's up, Mickey, Nellie?"

"Hey, KJ," Nellie and Mickey coo at once. My girls are so
weak when it comes to fine guys.

"What do we need to catch up on? Our sudden breakup or
this madness with Trecee?"

"I was hoping we could talk about something other than
that. Dang, Jayd, why you always gotta trip? I was just trying
to make conversation . . ."

"I don't need any conversation, KJ. What I need is solu-
tions. Do you have any? No . . . oh, then I guess this conversation is over. We can catch up after you get your broad off
my back."

"Uh, I don't mean to interrupt," Nellie says, sounding nervous, "but here comes your broad, KJ, and she doesn't look
like she wants to conversate with anybody."

And there Trecee is, looking like she's about to charge
both me and KJ.

"So, what's up, Jayd? Are you trying to talk to my man behind my back? Why you playin' with me, huh, Jayd?"

"Ain't nobody playin' with you, Trecee, and you need to step back. It's not that serious," I say, 'cause now she's really starting to piss me off. She's a real bold girl. She don't know me or my girls—we can get Compton crazy on her in a minute, but I decide to hold my composure, especially since she's not worth it.

"Trecee," KJ says, trying to calm her down. "Would you please just chill? Dang, it ain't even like that."

"Yes, it's that serious and it's just like that. And KJ, why are you protecting her? See, I knew you were trying to get back with him. You ain't fooling nobody, Jayd. This mess has to be settled now 'cause ain't nobody taking my man away from me, especially not no weird-ass girl like you."

Trecee starts to take off her fake gold earrings, rings, and nails. Here we go again. I don't move. I don't bat an eye. I just watch Trecee frantically take herself apart in front of everybody as she shouts all kinds of "unmentionables" at me, about me, and about what she's going to do to me for KJ, her man. It's safe to say talking ain't gone work with this chick. Mickey and Nellie were right.

"What's the matter with you, Trecee?" KJ asks, now standing between me and Trecee. "All I did was say hi to the girl, and now you swear we're about to walk down the aisle or something."

Trecee stopped to look at KJ. "Misty told me all about Jayd and her weird grandmother. She also told me that Jayd wants you back, even though she's been going around saying she ain't talking to you. You probably don't even know that girl bewitched you or something."

Bewitched him? Oh no, she didn't go there. If anybody is a witch, it's her. What the hell did Misty tell her? I know the broad's already crazy, but Misty made her go straight mental up in here. Where is Misty anyway?

"Come on, girl, there's the bell," Nellie says to me as KJ holds Trecee back.

"We'll walk you to class and make sure that witch don't come nowhere near you and I'll take you and Nellie home today so y'all don't have to worry about catching the bus," Mickey says.

Mickey has the straight gangsta girl mobile: a tweaked-out pink Regal with MICKEYS on her personalized license plates. She can be real cool in crisis situations. She should know how I feel. Girls in the neighborhood try to jump Mickey almost every time she comes out the door. That's why she stays in the house most of the time, if she's not with her man. I know she thinks I should fight, but she stands by my decision not to go there just yet.

"All right then, I'll meet y'all in the Main Hall after sixth period. I need to have a word with Misty before she leaves."

"For what, Jayd? What you need to do is beat her down and be done with it." Mickey's crazy and straight outta Compton. She'll fight anybody in a minute and, as pretty as Mickey is, she don't take no mess from nobody, no time. Usually, pretty girls don't like to get into fights for fear of messing up their hair or breaking their nails. But last year Misty got on Mickey's nerves talking behind her back. Mickey was whipping Misty so bad, Misty opted to run away instead of finish the fight. We weren't that close back then, but I'm glad Mickey is my friend now. I would hate to be her enemy.

"I want to see if she can go back and untell whatever lies she told Trecee in the first place. This is getting out of hand and I don't know what else to do. Dang, there goes the bell. I'll catch up with y'all after school, Main Hall."

I sure hope we can squash this mess. It's just getting bigger and bigger and I don't want to fight Trecee. It just doesn't seem valid enough to get suspended over. I still don't know exactly what Misty told Trecee, which is why I need to find her. I'll have to get out of class right before school lets out and snatch up Misty in the Main Hall.

Fifteen minutes before the end of the last period, I find, as predicted, Misty, the worst office aide ever, hangin' out in the hall not working, even though she should be working. When she sees me, she turns and walks in the other direction, but I catch up to her 'cause we're going to talk whether she likes it or not.

"Misty, we need to talk," I say when I'm close enough so she can't pretend not to hear me.

"Jayd, what you doin' out of class? And there is nothing for us to talk about."

"Then why you running from me, huh, Misty? Look, I don't know what kind of games you're playing, but the drama needs to end before somebody gets hurt. I know you told Trecee something to make her think I'm such a threat to her. Now I want to know what you said and I want you to tell her the truth."

Misty faces me with something like confidence. "I did tell her the truth. I told her that you're weird and you didn't hang out like the rest of us. I told her your grandmother be putting curses on people and stuff, and that's what my nana said and I know she ain't lyin' to me."

How could Misty be so vindictive and snide about this? Her nana ain't never even met Mama. She just heard about her like everybody else in the neighborhood. She went and told this girl a bunch of rumors and now the girl thinks I really did curse KJ into liking me. Oh damn, this is some real drama.

"Misty, if I could curse anybody, don't you think you'd be a cockroach by now?"

"Not funny, Jayd. Besides, my nana says you can't curse me because I've been in your house."

Misty's grandmother is as loony as they come. Straight up alcoholic, don't leave the garage, ain't seen daylight in years type of situation. Not a reliable source of information at all.

"What the hell does being in my house have to do with anything, Misty? This is a bunch of superstitious bull and you need to fix it or I will, and you won't be happy with the results, know what I'm sayin'?" She knows when she's gone too far and she knows I will take it there, if she pushes me.

"Fix this mess by Friday, Misty, or I *will* fix you."

"Jayd, don't threaten me. I have Trecee to back me up, remember? I ain't afraid of you."

"Yeah, not with her around, Misty, but I know where you live, where you hang out, where you don't hang out. Fix this by tomorrow. Don't play with me, Misty. I do have my ways of getting back at you."

And with that last threat, I was done talking to Misty. I was vexed and feeling hot, and I can't think straight when I get too hot. Thank God this day's almost over.

~ 15 ~
Wisdom Biscuits

*"Mama may have, Papa may have
But, God bless the child who's got his own."*

—BILLIE HOLIDAY

After I walk away from Misty, the bell rings. I decide to make my way to my locker when I run into Jeremy. "What's up, Jayd? How was the library?" he asks, falling in step with me as I walk down the hall. I don't know how to react. I'm fidgety and, while trying to shift my weight so I can hold my books, look cute, and talk to him at the same time, I drop all of my stuff right in front of him.

"Damn it!" I say, bending down to pick up my books, which are now strewn in the middle of the hall.

"Don't worry about it. Let me help you." Jeremy's a sweetie, I see. He kneels down and starts picking up errant books and papers.

"Thank you. I'm so clumsy sometimes. To answer your question, the library was cool. Better than being in class. Did I miss anything?" As I pick up the last of my things, I notice my girls walking toward me, laughing.

"Nah, you didn't miss nothing. Listen, I got to go to work. But, I want to talk to you about what you said in Government today. I like the way you handle that old hag," he says, smiling like a guilty little boy. "Here's my number. Can I get yours, too? I'll program it into my cell and give you a call when I get a chance." He handed me my English books and his phone number on an index card. I recite my cell number as he punches it into his phone. As Jeremy walks off, Nellie and Mickey arrive.

"Dang, Jayd. I never pegged you for the White boy type, but do your thizzle my nizzle," Mickey says, eyeing Jeremy as he walks down the hall.

"Mickey, you're too silly sometimes, though we did exchange numbers, and I will be calling him if he doesn't call me first." I put the stuff I don't need in my locker, grab my backpack, putting my homework and the necessary books inside, and close the locker door. I turn to face Nellie and Mickey, half expecting to see Trecee come my way. "Did y'all come up with any new ways to help me?" I ask as we walk down the hall toward the school parking lot.

"Girl, I don't know what to tell you. Can't your grandmother do something to help you?" Nellie asks, sounding a little scared for me.

"I've tried asking her for help. She only gave me a cleansing again and told me again how I was born, but I guess I'll try again." Mickey and Nellie look at me sympathetically, though I know they wonder about all the cleansings and Mama's potions. They haven't really asked, and I haven't really explained it all. Maybe one day.

When my girls drop me off at home, Mama's cooking. The warm scent of bell peppers engulfs the house and I'm instantly hungry.

On the way home, my girls and I talked and talked about the whole Misty–Trecee–KJ situation. All they could suggest was I be prepared for the fight. Mickey said she could get her boyfriend and his gangsta friends to come up there and back us up. Nellie suggested pepper spray for my defense. They're my girls and all, but when it comes to wisdom, Mama's where it's at, even if I don't understand all of what she tells me.

The best time to talk to Mama is when she's in her kitchen. Most nights after she cooks, she's on to *Jeopardy*, *Wheel of Fortune,* and then her private time, which consists of praying, chanting, cleaning her altar, and making remedies for her many clients.

Mama has her apron on, which is covered in flour and sugar and who knows what secret ingredients that make her biscuits so good. She's at her keenest in the kitchen. As she hands me some dough to knead, I ask her about her day.

I can tell she got her hair and nails done. Mama likes to wear her hair tied back in cornrows, sometimes in a bun. And her nails are immaculate. Never too long, never too short, her real nails are covered in acrylic. She says she does it to protect them from the cooking, but I say it's because she likes to get the fancy designs and airbrush polish. Yeah, she's something else.

As Mama turns around to get a biscuit cutter from the cabinet, I update her on my troubles. I tell her all about Trecee and Misty and KJ.

"Have you talked to KJ? I always did like that boy. He's so sweet and he's got a good heart. How are his folks?"

Mama likes everybody at first sight, especially if it's someone we're bringing home for her to meet. She'll smile big and bright and say, "Oh, my house is a mess and so am I. Chile, why you didn't tell me you were bringing company?" Then, she'll put on one of her best house robes and scarves, and go in the kitchen to bake something for the company to munch on.

"Yes, I've talked to KJ and I don't think there's much he

can do. She said I put some sort of curse on him to make him defend me. He tried to tell her that was nonsense, but she just kept going on and on about how he just didn't understand.

"Trecee says I'm strange and I'm trying to steal her man and make him strange too. But she's going to save him from me. Now the whole school wants to see this fight that I don't want to have."

"OK, Jayd, just take a deep breath. Now, you say this girl Trecee thinks you're strange and trying to take KJ away from her. Now, what would give her such a crazy idea?"

"Well, Misty told her—"

"Oh no, not Misty!" Mama says, rolling her eyes and throwing flour in the air.

"That girl is always in the middle of something. Always," Mama says, almost dropping a biscuit on the floor.

"She needs to get her own life. She's got plenty of drama in hers already, with her mama and grandma fighting all the damn time," I say, agreeing with Mama, or so I think.

"What did you say, young lady?" Mama asks in a low growl.

Mama is always swearing. When her sugar's up, she'll say, "Goddamn it, thank you Lord Jesus." But she won't let us cuss around her. I never could figure that one out. I tell Mama I was just agreeing with her and she chooses to let it go.

"That girl needs some help and some prayer," Mama continues, taking a deep breath and shaking her head from side to side. "Misty has always been jealous of you, Jayd, ever since you two got so close last year."

Just then, Mama dips the cut biscuits into a bowl of melted butter. She gently presses the biscuit with her fingers so the biscuits are completely submerged in butter. When the once-white biscuits are oozing with butter, Mama takes them out and places the perfectly round yellow biscuit onto the cookie sheet one by one. She hands me the rolling pin and cutting board so I can roll the dough until it's flat while she continues cutting and dipping the biscuits.

"Misty needs something else to worry over. That child's gonna end up in a whirlwind of trouble if she keeps messing with other people's lives like that. Just wait and see. That girl's gonna cross the wrong person one day, and her mouth won't help her then."

"Mama, I know I'm suppose to be patient with Misty, but she makes it so hard. I just don't know what I did to make Misty hate me so much or be so jealous of me."

Still cutting and dipping biscuits, Mama takes a big wooden spoon and scoops out a dollop of Crisco from the can. She places the Crisco in an already hot cast-iron skillet to fry some cube steak. I always like to watch the Crisco turn from solid white to crystal clear when it melts.

"Misty's jealousy has nothing to do with you. I'm sure she's had similar problems in the past. The best way to deal with Misty is to be as sweet and calm as you possibly can. Kill it with kindness, Jayd. Kill all evil by being as sweet as you possibly can."

The Crisco starts to pop in the skillet and Mama has just placed the last biscuit on the sheet. She takes the first piece of cube steak and places it in her "secret batter," which she uses to fry all meat.

"There's an order to everything. Like I always tell you, write your dreams down. Write down what you want to happen, even something like this school drama. If nothing else, writing may give you some clarity about the situation and even some peace of mind," Mama says, turning the meat until it's covered with batter and placing each piece strategically into the skillet.

After each piece of cube steak is safe in the hot frying pan, she places the biscuits in the oven. Then we start to work on the green beans, mashed potatoes, and gravy. Snapping beans is usually my favorite job to do, but Jay snapped all of the beans earlier this afternoon, since he gets home from school before I do. So I get to do my least favorite job—peeling hot potatoes.

As I take the first potato out of the pot my fingers begin to turn red from the steam. There is an art to peeling potatoes. If you're not careful and patient, you'll burn yourself. Trust me, I've burned myself several times.

"Just like them potatoes you peeling, Jayd, the situation you're in is hot and must be handled carefully. But everything hot will eventually cool off. Be patient, Jayd, and handle the situation so you don't end up being the one getting burned."

Speaking of burning things, how Mama knows when her buttermilk biscuits are ready is a mystery to me. When she takes them out of the oven they're always perfectly done—golden brown and nicely risen. Mama always gives me the first biscuit and with every bite I feel like all my troubles will just melt away. Maybe that's why I call them Wisdom Biscuits—after one of these, I know everything will be all right.

After eating dinner and doing both my school homework and Mama's homework, I can't fall asleep. I wonder if Jeremy's interested in more than just my smart mouth. How can I think about dating a new guy with all this mess around me?

When I get into bed, this mess with Trecee is still really bothering me. I don't want to wake up tomorrow and have to fight this girl. After tossing and turning, I finally fall asleep at about two in the morning, but only to dream about what was keeping me up in the first place, which is worrisome.

Because, like I said before, my dreams tend to prove true in one way or another. In this particular dream, Misty was walking through the main hall as she usually does during sixth period. She's the only office aide who's never actually in the office.

She sees KJ coming out of the boy's bathroom way down at the end of the hallway. She rushes toward him like she hasn't seen him in a long time. Misty's a big girl, if you know what I mean, so if she runs toward someone with the intent to jump on them, she'll probably hurt the person.

KJ doesn't know Misty's coming toward him as he starts walking back to class. Now she's just a few feet away from him. Her eyes are closed, her arms are out in front of her and in one hand she holds her hall pass. Her face is all squinted like she tasted something really foul, and her lips are puckered for the big kiss she's been waiting for.

Misty floors KJ and starts kissing him all over. KJ's so shocked and mortified he can't move. That's when Trecee walks in. As usual, even in my dream, the girl is ditching class and looking for somewhere to hide out.

Trecee sees Misty on top of KJ kissing her man in the middle of the hall. Trecee leaps into the air like a ninja and pounces Misty like a cat after its prey. And the fight is on.

I wake up to the alarm and Mama yelling, "Jayd, Jayd! Don't you hear that alarm, girl? Wake up!"

That was the end of my dream, but the beginning of a very, very long day at school. Misty and KJ? What the hell? Even in a dream the thought makes me sick.

I can't believe this. I can't believe it's already Friday morning and I'm supposed to be fighting this girl. Really, though, I'm not fighting anyone. That's what I've decided. If Trecee hits me, of course, I'll be forced to defend my precious assets, but I refuse to get suspended over this broad or KJ.

~ 16 ~
Misunderstandings and Half Truths

"It's all about the he said/she said bullshit."

—LIMP BIZKITS

It's another hot, sunny California day. I don't have any problems getting in the bathroom this morning, being that Bryan was out all night and still ain't made it home yet. The roosters from Esmeralda's yard are talking and Mr. Gatlin is watering his lawn. It's just another ordinary morning. So, why do I feel so weird? I've got to talk to KJ. Why do boys always get away with this stuff? I'm still waiting on the apology I'm owed for the way his trifling behind broke up with me. But, that's not what's on my mind today.

Trecee's on my mind. I must admit I'm nervous, but I ain't scared of her. She really is rather scrawny and weak and I'm sure she can't hurt me too bad. But, she's crazy and that does scare me. Crazy people are liable to do anything. I live with crazy people and they always scare the hell out of me, or at the very least surprise me. I know Trecee is full of surprises. I just hope she doesn't pull out too many tricks today.

First period

Spanish is always boring, especially because of my teacher, Mr. Donald. He's one of the football coaches, but is still forced to teach a class. I don't think he really speaks Spanish all that fluently, but this is the easiest class I have, so I take full advantage of it this morning. I decide to follow Mama's advice and write down this morning's dream. That's my second dream about a fight this week, both involving Misty. My nerves are shot, so I decide to write KJ a letter asking him to talk to Trecee for me. I even fold it into the shape of a shirt—his favorite letter shape—just to get in on his good side:

> *Dear KJ,*
>
> *What's up? Well, let's just get to the point, shall we? I don't know what's going on between you and Trecee. But the bottom line is, there ain't nothing going on between you and me anymore, and I would greatly appreciate you telling your new girl Trecee that. She's tripping hard and as you know she wants to fight me today. I know we're not on the best of terms, but you owe me something for the sorry way you broke up with me. The least you could do is set this broad straight and get her off my back. So, will you help me out, for old time's sake? I know you don't want to see your new girl get beat down—just kidding. Write back soon,*
>
> *Jayd*
>
> *Will you talk to Trecee?*
>
> *Check the Box*
>
> *Yes* ☐   *No* ☐

I'll deliver it to his second period class on the way to mine. I hope he writes back by break.

Second period

Where is this boy? He's usually not this late, but he would be on the day I need to see him. I can't be late to Mrs.

McDonnell's class. English is my favorite subject, and I don't want Mrs. McDonnell marking me tardy. I had her last year too so I know if I'm late she'll give me a look like she's been stabbed by her best friend. Then she'll say something like "to be late for one's own party is to miss the ball"—I don't really know what that means, but that's why I don't want to be late.

When she says something like that, probably some old quote she memorized in college, it'll be on your conscious all day because she's so cool about it. She says something weird like that and then just continues teaching. She never goes on long disciplinary tangents that make you mad. Yeah, she's good at the guilt trips.

"What's up, Jayd? Waiting for someone?" And finally, here's KJ—looking and smelling good as usual. That's why I can't get too close to this brother; reminds me of why I first fell in love with him.

"Oh, what's up, KJ? Here, I wrote this for your eyes only, all right? I gotta go, I don't want to be late for class. Please write me back by break. It's kind of urgent," I say, starting to run off to class.

"Dang, Jayd, why you acting all serious and bothered? Is this about Trecee? Look . . ."

I have to cut him off or get the McDonnell tardy quote, but I am very interested in what he had to say.

"Look, KJ, I have to go, but I do want to hear what you have to say. Meet me outside my English class after second period, all right?"

KJ looks surprised I cut him off. That's his problem; he always thinks people should just listen to him, no matter what. "All right, Jayd. You always were a feisty one. I'll see you at break."

As we go our separate ways, I think, *He better take care of this drama*. Oh dang, there goes the bell.

I make it to English just in time. She still gives me the

look, but no quote. "Class, how are we all this morning? I'm just wonderful."

Mrs. McDonnell must've had a morning cup of "joy" to get her off on the right foot. She's a tall White woman with bushy, curly, shoulder-length red hair. She's a tree-hugging, VW Bug-driving, moccasin–and–turquoise–wearing vegetarian, who's married to a Native American man, and has two daughters named Destiny and Karma. Strange, I know, but she's the best teacher I've ever met.

Mrs. McDonnell went to UCLA and then moved to Arizona to live on a reservation and study nature. What she ended up studying was her husband, John. He's fine. He picks her up every day after school in their beat-up VW. They've been married—and in love, she says—for fifteen years. I've never heard of that before—being "in love" for as long as you've been married. I know people who have been married for years, but I don't know that they've been in love the whole time.

Although I love her class, I ain't hearing Mrs. McDonnell this morning. All I can think about is KJ and the letter. I wonder what he'll say? I wonder if he'll remember his favorite letter shape? Why do I care so much?

Break

It's break and I'm out here waiting for this brotha, like the old days. KJ was a sweet and very attentive boyfriend, not out of the goodness of his heart, but because he likes to be "seen."

It was good for his status to be "seen" with me. As Misty says, "I'm a hard nut to crack, but everybody would like to take a shot at cracking me." I take pride in that. OK, here he comes, strutting like a pimp checking on his honeys. Uh-huh. He's so cocky sometimes it gets on my nerves. But he does look fine.

"What's up, Jayd? I read your little letter and I ain't checking no boxes. Let's go somewhere and talk," KJ says, handing me my note.

"Well, if you won't check the box, at least give me the answer to my question. Will you talk to Trecee for me or not?" Now, usually if KJ wants to say something he just says it in that sarcastic way of his and keeps on stepping. Well, not this time.

"Jayd, can we please go somewhere and talk about this? It's not as simple as you think. I can't just talk to Trecee. It's not that easy."

There's a look on his face that's got me scared—why isn't it that easy? He can't really be in love with this crazy broad. Is he afraid of her? Oh no, not another Maisha situation.

"Are you scared of her, KJ? You're so weak. First, I had to deal with you leaving me for Maisha, now this. When will you learn not to mess with these crazy broads just because they'll give up the cookies to you?"

KJ's looking around all anxious trying to usher me toward the door. "Jayd, keep your voice down and you don't know what you're talking about." KJ didn't just tell me that lie. If anybody knows about KJ's little indiscretions, if you will, it would be me. There's about to be a fight up in here, but it ain't gonna be between me and Trecee. It's going to be between me and this liar.

"Oh, so you didn't break up with me just because I wouldn't give it up?" I accuse, punching him as hard as I can in the arm. I've been waiting almost a week to have it out with him. Now's my chance.

"Tell me your sorry butt didn't break up with me because I wouldn't give you a taste, tell me it ain't true!" I say at the top of my lungs, still socking him. Students and teachers alike walk by staring at us, probably saying, "There goes another one of them out of control again." But, I don't give a damn. He deserves to be hurt as much as he hurt me.

"Damn, Jayd, calm down. Jayd, chill and stop hitting me before you force me to hurt you. Can we please go somewhere and talk about this? Jayd, stop!"

Just then, this boy grabs my wrist to keep me from my attack, spins me around, and pulls me into his arms. Oh no, he didn't. Dang, he smells good. I did forget how strong he is. Uh-oh, I think I might like this a little too much. He walks me over to the private quad behind the teacher's lounge where we used to hang out. Just me, him, and the other popular couples who wanted to make out without people staring.

"KJ, can we go somewhere else to talk? This brings back too many bad memories for me," I say, rolling my eyes and sucking my teeth. He's too good at playing with my emotions. Maybe Bryan was right.

"Jayd, is there a better place you can think of to talk privately? No, I didn't think so. So, will you please cut out all the drama so we can talk like two rational people."

"Fine, KJ, let's start with why you can't—or won't—talk to Trecee for me. What's that all about?"

"Jayd, maybe you're right about me dealing with crazy broads just because they give it up. Trecee says she's pregnant and that I'm the daddy. She's pregnant, but I don't believe it's my baby. We used protection and everything. Now she's going around acting like it's my baby she's having and she's making my life crazy. Can you believe this mess?"

"No, KJ, I can't."

I can't believe I was able to manage even those words. I could hardly make a sound. Trecee pregnant with KJ's baby? This can't be happening. If I know one thing about him, it's that KJ believes fiercely in protection, so obviously she's lying. Every time he would try to get in my panties, he always had a Trojan Magnum right by his side. But, what if she's not lying? What then? KJ is a senior on his way to one of the top colleges on a full basketball scholarship I'm sure. She ain't that stupid—and she knew what she was doing when she landed KJ in bed.

"So, you see, Jayd, it's not that simple. It's a whole lot of drama with this one. I don't know what to do. I thought about going to see your grandmother and get some guidance, some food, some something."

I had to laugh at that. When KJ would invite me over to his house, Mama always made him a plate of food to go. Mama says there's all types of magic in food. KJ would offer me some as he led me through his house to sit on his swinging porch chairs in his parent's backyard. Usually, I'd take only a single bite before he'd systematically kill off every other drop of food on his plate. He loves Mama's cooking.

"I need some help, Jayd, and I don't know where to go. I can't tell my parents. If they find out, they'll flip. Oh, my dad would be so upset. And my mom would be very disappointed in me. And I know, this ain't all about me. I'm sorry she dragged you into this, Jayd."

Now I do feel kind of sorry for him and I wish he had come to me a little bit sooner, like before the day of the fight. It's not like we can run home to Mama now. She may have known what to do had she had a little more information. Maybe that's what Mama meant when she said that it's not really my drama. But I still don't understand how I got in the middle of his mess.

"KJ, I feel for you and all, but I still don't know how, exactly how, I ended up a participant in your baby mama drama."

"That's not funny, Jayd. This is a very serious situation. You ended up in it because I made the mistake of telling Trecee the truth," he says, looking around the quad like a paranoid pothead. There's no one here now but us.

"And exactly what truth did you tell her, KJ? Trecee's truth is that I still want you and that's a lie. What did you tell her, Kalvinice Alonzo Jenkins Jr.?" I had to call him out. He's too used to drawing on sympathy to get out of stuff. But not this time. This time he was going to be a man about this and take responsibility for his actions. If I have to call him out like his mama, then so be it.

"Hey, girl, don't be calling me by my full name. Don't nobody else over here know it and I want to keep it that way."

"Whatever, KJ. I just want to know the truth. What did you tell Trecee to make her come after me like this?"

"Okay, but first you have to understand the situation. We were in the car one night playing Truth or Dare. It was my turn and I was afraid of her next dare, so I chose truth—worst choice of my life. Anyway, Trecee asked me if I had ever been in love and if so, with who. I said, yes, and with Jayd."

Just as my heart stops beating and my jaw drops to the ground, the bell rings for the end of break and the beginning of third period. What the hell kind of mind games is he up to now?

"Look, KJ," I say, trying to sound as cool and as unbothered as possible. "I don't care what you said to Trecee to make her go psycho on me. I just know that it needs to end, cease, stop and now. So, do something."

"Jayd, what can I do? Trecee's not the most rational person. I tried to talk to her about this drama between you and her, but she won't hear me. She's convinced you cast a love spell on me and I don't mean it when I stick up for you. She's not stable, Jayd, and I'm sorry about all of this but I don't know what else to do or say."

"Yeah, you're sorry all right. You're the sorriest brotha I've ever known. First you can't control yourself. Now you can't control your broads. I'm sorry I ever went with you. You have been nothing but a major source of drama and pain in my life. I don't even know why I thought you could help me. You can't even help yourself."

Just like that, I got up to walk to math class. This was a waste of time and energy. He's so full of himself, thinking 'cause he said he's in love with me that I'm gonna just melt and forget this girl is supposed to be beating my ass by the end of the day. He's something else.

"Jayd, don't be like that," he says, grabbing my right hand from my thigh and putting it on his lap. "Look, I'm not going to let anything happen to you, especially not because of me. I'm serious, Jayd," he says, looking straight into my eyes.

Why is he touching me? I hate when he grabs my hand; it weakens my "mad" defenses. Not so easily this time, though. I'm too worried about Trecee and about being late to Mr. Ball's class. I hate math, but I'm sure I'll hate it even more if I'm late.

"Peace, KJ, I'll see you later. I don't want to be late for class."

"Come on, let me at least walk you," he says, getting up to follow me.

"Fine, but don't talk to me unless it's to tell me you found a way to get Trecee off of my case by the end of the day," I say, still not giving in to him.

"Is that all you can say?" KJ asks.

"Right now, yes. That's all that's on my mind. Thank you for walking me to class," I say. Luckily my class is right around the corner from the teachers' lounge, so he doesn't have much time to sell me any more of his bull.

"Look, can we have lunch together? I think we still need to talk, don't you?"

KJ touches my face. We do have some unfinished business to attend to. And he'll take me off campus—and pay. "Fine,

KJ, lunch doesn't sound too bad. Meet me outside of Mrs. Peterson's class—oh, that's right. I've been 'banned' from her wack class until I finish writing the Constitution."

"Dang, Jayd, what did you do this time?"

"Never mind that. Just meet me outside the library after fourth period, and make sure Trecee doesn't see us."

"All right, you bet. I'll be there. I have Leadership fourth and we usually get out early. So I'll be there right when the bell rings."

As the tardy bell rings and KJ sprints down the hall, I have to ask myself what I'm doing. I feel like Ashanti—foolish. I must be a fool to trust KJ again. What does he want to talk about anyway? I know what I have to say, and he's not going to like it. I just want him to know exactly how much he hurt me and how shady it was for him to do it over the phone. I want him to know he's a punk and that he doesn't deserve me. And I want him to know how much I loved him and that I would've given it up to him had he just waited a little longer. Oh well, too late now, especially since he's gone be a daddy. But I still want to hear what this punk has to say.

~ 17 ~
The Fight

Third period

"**G**ood morning, class. Please take out your books and turn to page thirty-six. Do all the problems on the page and turn it in at the end of class." I don't hate math for the sake of hating it. I hate math because all the math teachers here are awful. They don't teach or explain anything, at least not any of the ones I've been so fortunate to encounter.

Mr. Ball is a short, round, bald-headed man who laughs at his own pathetic jokes, and knows only what he knows, and nothing more. If you ask him questions, he refers you to the book. Once when I had him last year, this man gave me a pass to go ask another teacher to explain it to me. He says I ask too many questions to be a good math student. I say it's because I have a bad math teacher. But no sense in complaining. I still have to do the work to get out of here, so I might as well get used to it. I take out my book and my notebook.

Scott, the class leech, leans forward from the desk behind me to ask, "Hey, Jayd, can I borrow a pencil?"

"I don't have an extra pencil, Scott." I say, telling the truth. I hate writing in pencil, so I only keep one in my math notebook. No extras.

"Well, can I borrow a piece of paper, then?" he asks. Now I'm annoyed. I turn around to look at him.

"Scott, why don't you bring supplies to class? Do you not know that you'll need your book, paper, and a pencil every-day?" I say, loud enough for everyone in the room to hear.

"Damn, Jayd, what's up with you this morning? Oh, I know. That girl with the braids is going to kick your ass today. Yeah, I heard about that," Scott says with a sadistic grin on his face. The other students look up from their work to see my reaction.

"Shut the hell up, with your freeloading punk ass." I turn back to my work, avoiding eye contact with everyone else. I can't let this White boy get to me. I got too much other stuff on my mind.

"Okay, you two, settle down and get to work," Mr. Ball says from his desk.

Settle down? How can I do that with all of this drama going on? I wonder if teachers even notice when students are having bad days.

Fourth period

Since I'm still banned from Government, I go to find soli-tude in the library. At first I thought this was the worst pun-ishment Mrs. Peterson could have given me. But, I must say that chillin' in the library does give me some peace amidst all the chaos. But, the universe has other plans today.

When I turn down the hall to walk toward the east quad where the library and computer lab are, I run right into Misty walking up the hall.

"Hey, Jayd, you look a little green—everything all right?"

I choose to ignore her petty behind and walk past her when I hear someone call my name from a distance. Is that KJ? I turn around to see him running toward me.

"Jayd, I'm glad I caught up with you. Let me walk you to

the library. Oh, what's up, Misty?" KJ says, almost knocking her over.

Looking shocked and confused, but no doubt interested, Misty says, "Hey, KJ," like she's auditioning for a Jay-Z video.

KJ basically looks through Misty and ignores her obvious attempt to flirt with him; he smiles at me.

"Come on, Jayd. Let's get going before the bell rings," KJ says, grabbing my hand and leading me toward the east quad.

"Bye, KJ. Oh, and I'll tell Trecee you said hello," Misty says.

"Yeah, you do that, Misty. No doubt you'll put your extras on it," KJ responds.

Giggling, but no doubt feeling foolish, she says, "KJ, you're so funny. I'll talk to you later, OK?"

And with that last pathetic attempt at capturing his attention, Misty's gone.

"Jayd, let's ditch fourth and go somewhere and kick it. We need to solve this and it's going to take longer than lunch to even get started."

"I don't know, KJ. I'm already in deep with Mrs. Peterson and I don't want to get in over my head."

"She'll never know. Besides, Jayd, what's she gonna do—come out of her full class to check on you? I don't think so. Let's go to Alonzo's and split a burrito and talk about what's really going on—between me and you."

Now how could I say no to half a burrito and a charming smile?

I forgot how good a burrito is with KJ. He gets the works, something I would never do. When he splits a burrito with me, it's actually not in half. It's usually one-quarter for me and three-quarters for him. As big as they are, this is the perfect ratio for us.

After we place our order, we sit down at a booth outside.

From our seats we're able to see the sparkling blue ocean water. I remember the first time we came here we walked to the beach after we ate. It was the nicest lunch date I've ever had. Speaking of us, KJ didn't waste any time getting to his point.

"Look, Jayd, after all that's gone down between us this summer, I just want to set the record straight. I don't love Trecee, and I never did or will. I only love one girl and that's you."

He thinks his game is slick and airtight, but it doesn't work on me. Some cat telling me he loves me is not enough to make me go running back to him. I still remember how he treated me at the end of our relationship. If he thinks I'm letting him off this easy, after all the drama I've been through and am still going through because of him, he's got another thing coming.

"KJ, why are you telling me this now? You just move at lightning speed, don't you? One girl to the next, just like that without a second thought. What's wrong with you? This girl is crazy over you, willing to jump me to prove that to you, and yet you're here telling me you love me. What kind of twisted game are you playing now?"

KJ looks hurt and leans in closer to take my hand. "First of all, it ain't one girl to the next. I ain't no dog like you think I am, Jayd."

"Whatever, KJ. You went from Maisha to me to Trecee. It's just a game to you, and yet all the girls end up hurt and involved in a bunch of mess over you and it ain't fair."

It isn't fair. Not to any of the girls involved in this mess. I know so many sistahs who get played like this all the time, and they always end up going back to the cat. Like all he did is irrelevant because now, he truly loves me and this time it'll be different. No, not this sistah, not this time.

"Jayd, I know you're angry with me and hurt and upset. If

I were you, I wouldn't want to talk to me again either—at first. But, that's if you only remember the end of our relationship. Before that, it was really good, or at least I thought so. We were hella tight, Jayd, and I want that again."

OK, now either his game is improving, or I still have feelings for this brotha. I need some air to think. This is just too much excitement for one day.

"KJ, maybe we should be getting back to campus."

"We haven't even had our food yet," he protests.

"Yeah, but I need to meet my girls."

"Don't look like we need to go back to see your girls. Here they come now."

Sure enough, Nellie and Mickey are pulling into Alonzo's parking lot waving me down.

"Jayd, girl, come on. Get in the car. Trecee is trying to get a ride here to come get you," Nellie says, hanging out of Mickey's car window.

"Yeah, Misty conveniently came into fourth period and told Trecee you and KJ went off campus together for lunch at your old spot. Misty can put a lot on stuff sometimes, can't she though?"

Mickey got that right. Misty and her big, wicked mouth. She'll never learn to stay out of my business. That's who I feel like fighting, if anybody. She's not getting away with this. Just as I get up from the booth to hop into Mickey's ride, my heart begins to race. I feel like I'm going to explode and then I remember my dream about fighting Misty.

"Come on, y'all, let's go back to school. I'm so tired of running from these broads. If they want to fight me, so be it. But neither one of them is getting away with this."

"I knew Misty was going to run to Trecee and tell her she saw us together," KJ says. "I'm going to get our burrito and meet y'all at the school."

"KJ, how can you be worried about food at a time like

this?" I ask, a little bitter that he's still thinking about eating when his baby mama is on her way up here to start some mess with me.

"Jayd, ain't nothing gone happen," he says, turning toward the counter to pick up our order. "Besides, a brotha still got to eat, right?"

"Right, KJ," I say, snatching our burrito from his hands and throwing it in the trash before getting in the car with my girls.

"Enjoy your lunch," I shout. Mickey pulls off.

"Damn, Jayd, what you do that for?" KJ yells after me as Mickey's ride takes us back to Drama High.

After lunch

When we get to the campus, the air is charged. I hate that fight feeling. Nothing good ever comes out of a fight and I know that someone is about to have one. Lunch is over and fifth period is already in progress.

"Don't worry, Jayd. You know we got your back," Nellie says, with her hand on my shoulder.

"Jayd, I just want to say again that I'm sorry you got dragged into this mess. I ain't letting Trecee do nothing to you, I promise," KJ says, eating the second burrito he ordered after we left. It took him a minute to catch up to us. Mickey took her time getting back to campus, stopping to get me some Vaseline for my face just in case I have to take a couple of blows to the head.

It's sweet of KJ to offer his protection, but this is personal now. Misty's lying and twisting things up in Trecee's little mind, and it's time for it to all be untwisted. And, there Trecee is, waiting for me by the main gate. My heart is racing and my head is hot. Yeah, I'm a little scared, but it's about to be on up in here.

. . . I'm a little scared, but it's about to be on up in here.

Just as I'm ready to face my opponent head-on, I begin sweating like I'm in Miami during carnival, and jarring another déjà vu experience; then I remember the dream I had about a fight with Misty. A little shaken, but still determined to teach Trecee a lesson she'll never forget, I walk over to the main gate, with my girls in tow. We're ready for whatever comes our way. But before I even get close to Trecee, Shae comes out of nowhere with her man Tony right behind her.

"Hey, Jayd, what's up, girl? I got a little info you might be interested in," she says. Then she yells over to Trecee, "You too, Trecee. Although you gone end up feeling real stupid after I say what I gotta say."

What are Shae and Tony doing here? They act like the bell for fifth period didn't ring a few minutes ago. Doesn't anybody care about going to class anymore?

"Look, Shae, this ain't got nothing to do with you so why don't you step back and let me handle this," Trecee says while moving toward me. I'm ready for her. I take off my earrings and rings and hand them to Nellie. Usually I wouldn't fight a pregnant girl. But for all I know she could be lying and I ain't gone sit here and let her kick my ass. I'll be as careful as I can.

Mickey's talking mad stuff. "Trecee, you ain't nothing but trash and you been jealous of my girl all along," she says. "You was just looking for a reason to fight, and now you gone get your ass whipped."

"You don't have to do this, Jayd. You can still walk away," Nellie says, looking from me to Trecee and back at me.

"It's too late for reasoning with this broad, Nellie."

As I take off my backpack and hand it to Nellie, the "No More Drama" bag Mama gave me on Tuesday falls to the ground. Where the hell did this come from? As I bend down to pick it up, I notice it has the word LISTEN written on the side. There are no coincidences, so I decide to let Shae have her say.

"What's up, Shae? What's so important you have to speak on it now?"

"Well, normally I wouldn't break up no fight, but this is a little different. Misty has been playin' both of y'all in this little game of hers. She's trying to get KJ all to herself. She told my home girl Trina yesterday she made up all this BS about Jayd and fed it to Trecee, who is stupid anyway, and she was gone get Jayd beat up and Trecee kicked out, and that would leave KJ all to her."

"What? Why would she think that? She ain't got no chance with me," KJ says, stepping up and looking dumbfounded.

"Well, Misty has never been too smart, now has she, KJ?" I say to him, not knowing what else to say.

"And, as for you, Trecee," Shae continues, "you know good and well that your baby ain't KJ's. You were pregnant before you started messing with KJ, and I know who the baby's daddy is, so you need to stop trippin' and leave them alone. It's Misty you need to be concerned with."

"Pregnant?" Nellie and Mickey exclaim in unison. KJ puts his head in his hands and just starts saying, "Thank you, Jesus" over and over again.

After Shae finishes with her exposè, she and her silent man turn around and leave just as quickly as they came. Then we all start looking for Misty. Usually, I wouldn't want to fight Misty because I do feel kind of sorry for her. But this time is an exception. When I find her I'm going to teach her a lesson she'll never forget.

Unfortunately for her though, I don't see her before Trecee does, and the next thing I know, Trecee's running toward Misty at full speed. Me, my girls, and KJ run after Trecee, anxious to see what she'll say or do.

"What's up, Trecee? I had to get a bathroom pass to get out of fifth period. Did I miss the fight?" Misty asks with a big Kool-Aid smile on her face.

"No. You're just in time."

Just as Trecee says the word "time," she slaps that smile clean off of Misty's face and punches her to the ground. When we get there we can only sit back and watch. Misty deserves every lick she can take from Trecee. If the security guards hadn't rushed over when they did, Misty would have been stomped to the ground.

"Break it up girls, break it up!" Dan and Stan say. But, it's obvious they're not used to dealing with Black girls fighting 'cause that ain't gone work.

Trecee has Misty in a headlock and is pulling her hair while Misty is screaming for her life.

"I'm sorry! I'm sorry, Trecee. I was just trying to help."

"Help, my ass! Shae told me everything, you lying wench. Lie now. I can't hear you. What you say? Everything that comes out of your mouth is a lie. And I'm going to shut your mouth for good," Trecee says while still holding Misty in a headlock.

Now the guards get serious and pull them apart, which isn't easy. Trecee keeps getting away from Dan to get a couple more shots in on Misty, who is just stupefied by the whole thing.

As for the rest of us, we get hauled off to the principal's office for ditching class. It could have been much worse, and I'm just thankful that it wasn't me in the fight after all. I'm just too cute to be fighting over some BS. No, not Miss Jayd Jackson. But, I ain't done with Misty yet—not by a long shot.

Epilogue

I think it's safe to say I won't have to worry about Trecee no time soon. She's been permanently expelled from South Bay High. This school won't hesitate to ship your behind out quick, fast, and in a hurry if you cause too much trouble. In Trecee's case, this was the straw that broke the camel's back if you hear what I'm sayin'.

She's only been here for less than a year, and has already been suspended, put on probation, and almost arrested and now expelled. So, I guess she won't be having KJ's illegitimate baby after all. Yeah, I'm glad the broad is gone. She's definitely crazy.

As for Misty, she's only crazy when she gets bored and an opportunity to start some mess comes along. I have a feeling she'll always be around somewhere—either at the mall, or the beauty shop, or around the corner. We do live down the street from each other. And now she likes KJ. What kind of mess is this going to start?

Mickey already heard Misty rode home with KJ after school, even after he said Misty didn't have a chance. I don't really care. I already told everybody I don't like KJ's old sweaty, musty, basketball-playing punk behind anymore. Now, Misty's trying to get with him. I can't believe this madness.

They can't be serious. This must be a bunch of Misty's made-up drama, or is it? Anyways, I've been thinking more and more about this cutey Jeremy. At first I was tripping hard because he's White and Jewish. But now, especially after dealing with this mess, I think I might just entertain the thought of calling him tonight, since he hasn't called me yet. I need a break from the norm.

Forget KJ. After all he's put me through, why should I even give him the time of day? I need a man to treat me good for once. Not be no dog. Someone I ain't got to worry about seeing at the mall with some other broad, know what I'm sayin'?

My girls—and all the other females at this school with any taste—think Jeremy's the cutest boy up here, Black, White, or other. I remember the first time I saw him I thought, "Damn, that White boy is *fine!*"

But what will everyone think? Me, Miss Sassy, all about Compton, Black power Jayd Jackson dating a White boy? I can just hear the gossip now, "She sold out. She think she too good for Black folks now. She always was like that." They already talk enough about me not belonging to South Central, so I guess I really shouldn't care what they think.

It's just another Friday back at home. Mama's in her spirit room, making potions for her clients; Daddy's at church for Bible study. Jay is in his room watching TV, and all of my uncles are gone, as usual.

I grab my Hefty bags out the closet and get out the weekend stuff I bring to my mom's. I usually pack a couple of outfits just in case I go out with my girls, my hair stuff, my work clothes, and my CDs and books. I also have homework to finish for Mama still, so I guess I better get my spirit notebook too.

"Jayd, get your stuff and let's go. I got a date tonight," my mom yells from the back porch. My mom's never on time picking me up and is always rushing me when she finally does get here.

"Lynn, stop rushing that girl. She had a hard day," Mama shouts from her spirit room.

"Hi, Mama," my mom yells back. "There's a lot of traffic on the 405 and I have to be somewhere by eight o'clock."

"Well, you still got two hours. Why don't you come back here and help me for a minute?" Mama says, knowing my mom ain't going nowhere near her spirit room.

"That's okay, Mama. I'll pass. Jayd, get your butt out here and let's go," my mom says, walking to her car parked in the driveway. I'm right behind her, after blowing a kiss to Mama through the door of her spirit room.

"I love you girls and be safe!" Mama yells.

"I love you too, Mama. Good night," I say, throwing my garbage bag–turned–luggage into the backseat of my mom's Mazda.

I hope I get to talk to Jeremy tonight. All I know is that if he asks me out, I'm saying yes, no matter what KJ, Misty, or anybody else thinks. I'm sure there will be a lot of talk behind that one. Oh well, we don't call this Drama High for nothing.

Drama High, Volume 1:
THE FIGHT

L. Divine

ABOUT THIS GUIDE

The following questions are intended to enhance
your group's reading of
DRAMA HIGH: THE FIGHT
by L. Divine.

DISCUSSION QUESTIONS

1. In what ways is Jayd a typical teenager? In what ways is she different? Do her life experiences in any way mirror anything that's happened in your life or someone you know?

2. Why did Trecee want to fight Jayd? Was she right to challenge Jayd? How would you have handled the situation in Jayd's place?

3. Do you know a girl at your school or in your neighborhood that reminds you of Trecee? What makes someone like Trecee behave the way she does?

4. What role did KJ play in the drama between Trecee and Jayd? Does he bear any responsibility for Trecee's behavior?

5. Do you know a boy at school or in your neighborhood that reminds you of KJ? What makes someone like KJ behave the way he does?

6. Were Jayd's friends Mickey and Nellie helpful to her as she tried to think her way out of the fight? What advice would you have given to Jayd?

7. Jayd says every girl has another girl who hates on her? For Jayd, that girl is Misty. Is there a Misty in your life? Are you a Misty? How do you handle the Mistys of the world?

8. Who are your friends more like: Mickey, Nellie, or Misty?

9. What are the differences between Mickey, Nellie, and Misty? What traits do each have that benefit Jayd? What traits do each have that are a disadvantage?

10. Nellie is slightly more well-off than Jayd and Mickey. How does this affect the trio's friendship? Can money come between friends? When can this happen?

11. Which character are you most like?

12. Like a lot of teens, Jayd is being raised by her grand-

mother Mama. But Jayd's grandmother isn't like the typical grandmother. She carries on the mystical traditions of African-American culture. This is a big part of Jayd's life and upbringing. How does this help and hinder Jayd? How similar are Jayd's family traditions to yours?

13. Jayd attends and all-White school. Would you attend a school that was predominately attended by one race over another? Would you attend a school that was predominately attended by a race different than your own? What are the advantages and disadvantages?

14. What kind of school do you attend? Is it anything like Drama High? Would you like to go to a school like Drama High?

15. What sort of drama can go on any given day at your school? Do you tend to avoid the drama or are you responsible for starting the drama? Are there any circumstances under which drama can be a good thing?

Start Your Own Book Club

Courtesy of the DRAMA HIGH series

ABOUT THIS GUIDE

The following is intended to help you get
the Book Club you've always wanted
up and running!
Enjoy!

Start Your Own Book Club

A Book Club is not only a great way to make friends, but it is also a fun and safe environment for you to express your views and opinions on everything from fashion to teen pregnancy. A Teen Book Club can also become a forum or venue to air grievances and plan remedies for problems.

The People

To start, all you need is yourself and at least one other person. There's no criteria for who this person or persons should be other than having a desire to read and a commitment to discuss things during a certain time frame.

The Rules

Just as in Jayd's life, sometimes even Book Club discussions can be filled with much drama. People tend to disagree with each other, cut each other off when speaking, and take criticism personally. So, there should be some ground rules:

1. Do not attack people for their ideas or opinions.
2. When you disagree with a book club member on a point, disagree respectfully. This means that you do not denigrate other people for their ideas or even their ideas, themselves, i.e., no name calling or saying, "That's stupid!" Instead, say, "I can respect your position, however, I feel differently."
3. Back up your opinions with concrete evidence, either from the book in question or life in general.
4. Allow every one a turn to comment.
5. Do not cut a member off when the person is speaking. Respectfully wait your turn.
6. Critique only the idea (and do so responsibly; saying, "That's stupid!" is not allowed). Do not criticize the person.

7. Every member must agree to and abide by the ground rules.

Feel free to add any other ground rules you think might be necessary.

The Meeting Place

Once you've decided on members, and agreed to the ground rules, you should decide on a place to meet. This could be the local library, the school library, your favorite restaurant, a bookstore, or a member's home. Remember, though, if you decide to hold your sessions at a member's home, the location should rotate to another member's home for the next session. It's also polite for guests to bring treats when attending a Book Club meeting at a member's home. If you choose to hold your meetings in a public place, always remember to ask the permission of the librarian or store manager. If you decide to hold your meetings in a local bookstore, ask the manager to post a flyer in the window announcing the Book Club to attract more members if you so desire.

Timing is Everything

Teenagers of today are all much busier than teenagers of the past. You're probably thinking, "Between chorus rehearsals, the Drama Club, and oh yeah, my job, when will I ever have time to read another book that doesn't feature Romeo and Juliet!" Well, there's always time, if it's time well-planned and time planned ahead. You and your Book Club can decide to meet as often or as little as is appropriate for your bustling schedules. *Once a month* is a favorite option. *Sleepover Book Club* meetings—if you're open to excluding one gender—is also a favorite option. And in this day of high-tech, savvy teens, *Internet Discussion Groups* are also an appealing option. Just choose what's right for you!

Well, you've got the people, the ground rules, the place, and the time. All you need now is a book!

The Book

Choosing a book is the most fun. THE FIGHT is of course an excellent choice, and since it's a series, you won't soon run out of books to read and discuss. Your Book Club can also have comparative discussions as you compare the first book, THE FIGHT, to the second, SECOND CHANCE, and so on.

But depending upon your reading appetite, you may want to veer outside of the Drama High series. That's okay. There are plenty of options, many of which you will be able to find under the Dafina Books for Young Readers Program in the coming months.

But don't be afraid to mix it up. Nonfiction is just as good as fiction and a fun way to learn about from where we came without just using a history text book. Science fiction and fantasy can be fun, too!

And always, always research the author. You might find the author has a website where you can post your Book Club's questions or comments. The author may even have an e-mail address available so you can correspond directly. Authors will also sit in on your Book Club meetings, either in person, or on the phone, and this can be a fun way to discuss the book as well!

The Discussion

Every good Book Club discussion starts with questions. THE FIGHT, as will every book in the Drama High series, comes along with a Reading Group Guide for your convenience, though of course, it's fine to make up your own. Here are some sample questions to get started:

1. What's this book all about anyway?
2. Who are the characters? Do we like them? Do they remind us of real people?
3. Was the story interesting? Were real issues of concern to you examined?
4. Were there details that didn't quite work for you or ring true?
5. Did the author create a believable environment—one that you could visualize?
6. Was the ending satisfying?
7. Would you read another book from this author?

Record Keeper

It's generally a good idea to have someone keep track of the books you read. Often libraries and schools will hold reading drives where you're rewarded for having read a certain number of books in a certain time period. Perhaps, a pizza party awaits!

Get Your Teachers and Parents Involved

Teachers and parents love it when kids get together and read. So involve your teachers and parents. Your Book Club may read a particular book where it would help to have an adult's perspective as part of the discussion. Teachers may also be able to include what you're doing as a Book Club in the classroom curriculum. That way books you love to read such as the Drama High ones can find a place in your classroom alongside the books you don't love to read so much.

Resources

To find some new favorite writers, check out the following resources. Happy reading!

Young Adult Library Services Association
http://www.ala.org/ala/yalsa/yalsa.htm

Carnegie Library of Pittsburgh
Hip-Hop!
Teen Rap Titles
http://www.carnegielibrary.org/teens/read/booklists/teen-rap.html

TeensPoint.org
What Teens Are Reading?
http://www.teenspoint.org/reading_matters/book_list.asp?sort=5&list=274

Teenreads.com
http://www.teenreads.com/

Sacramento Public Library
Fantasy Reading for Kids
http://www.saclibrary.org/teens/fantasy.html

Book Divas
http://www.bookdivas.com/

Meg Cabot Book Club
http://www.megcabotbookclub.com/

Getting to Know L. Divine

Drama High is a truly unique animal in teen fiction. Aside from Cheetah Girls, very few series prominently feature African-American characters or the life experiences. Is this what inspired you to write Drama High?

Exactly. I saw the lack of interest from the Black student population in the fiction they were given to read in school, as well as what's available at the bookstores and libraries. As both a former student and educator, I wanted to create a series featuring Black teens like the ones I knew—like the teen I had been. I also wanted to give a voice to the seemingly never-ending drama of the high school years—our way. Thus, the creation of Jayd and her Drama High crew.

Who is L. Divine? Why pen name?

L. Divine is a combination of my nickname, Lysa, and my self-given last name Divine, like X. I really don't see it as a pen name since most people call me either Lysa or Divine. It's just one of my spiritual names, if you will.

Also, how does spirituality operate in your life?

My spirituality is my life. It's very personal and private and it's the center of my family structure. Everything I do and receive is ordained by the Creator and I am a manifestation of that energy, which I recognize through my reflection as Osun. It's also echoed in my name, L. Divine. Instead of choosing an unknown letter to signify my ancestry's lineage, I chose Divine because if I know one thing for sure, it's that I (and everything else in creation) am of God or divine. I know for a fact that without my spirituality, I wouldn't be here to share my stories.

Jayd is an intriguing character. She's street savvy, outspoken, and, for a sixteen-year-old from the hood, she's very wise. Yet at the same time, you still manage to portray the girl in her. But what really sets Jayd apart from her peers, other characters in competing series, and the readers you hope to attract? In what ways is she similar?

Unlike the girls in other series such as *The Sisterhood of the Traveling Pants* or *The Gossip Girls*, Jayd's Black, from Compton, and dedicated to her education. She's also true to her African-American roots, proud to be an individual thinker, and loves herself just the way she is. Jayd's similar because she still has the same problems that other adolescent girls have, like finding the perfect jeans or choosing the right boyfriend.

Jayd and her grandmother have mystical powers and knowledge. What does this element bring to the series, and why is it important to you to portray this side of their life in your book?

It's important for young readers to experience the many different facets of African-American culture. All of us aren't churchgoing folk and most of our grandmothers and great-grandmothers do have connections to the ancient spiritual ways of our ancestors. I just wanted to portray this side of our culture too. This theme is also an element in the writings of Gayl Jones and Octavia Butler and is a tradition that should be continued in literature even for our young readers. Otherwise, it is a tradition that is lost.

What other young adult authors do you read?

I love the Harry Potter series by J.K. Rowling, as well as the older Francine Pascal series, *Sweet Valley High*. I also like the newer series such as *The Cheetah Girls*, as well as *The Sisterhood of the Traveling Pants*.

Describe the perfect writing environment.

For inspiration and new material, I have lunch at a restaurant and food store I mention in the book, Simply Wholesome, in Los Angeles. For refinement and revision, I sit in my big comfy chair at my makeshift desk/dining room table.

Who is the one person living or dead that you would like to have dinner with? Why?

It's honestly a tie between my two favorite writers, Octavia Butler and Alice Walker. Both women portray the essence of creativity and exemplify the use of your divine talent to heal yourself and give jewels to our world. I own just about every book they've written and I find inspiration not only in their words, but also in their chosen paths.

If you could have one superpower, what would it be? Why?

To change the past. Well, I don't believe in living with regrets. I regret a lot of the choices I've made in my life and anticipate more to come; that's just the process of life. It's a good thing and some choices that seem bad in retrospect are actually blessings in disguise. But, I would like to have the choice to take back what I want, when I want. So, that's the most valuable superpower I can think of: the ability to not only learn from my mistakes, but to then go back and change my mind after the fact. A lot of people's lives would be different, as well as my own.

Stay tuned for the next book in this series
SECOND CHANCE,
available December 2006
wherever books are sold.
Until then, satisfy your "Drama High" craving
with the following excerpt from the next installment.

ENJOY!

Prologue

OK, I still can't believe they suspended all of us, even though my girls and I didn't want to be fightin' in the first place. Ain't that just wrong? You see what I mean about people just straight hatin' on us up here? I swear. Well, I'm glad we're at South Bay High and not some school in the hood. These schools have no problem calling the police on you or kicking you out on the spot for something like this.

We didn't even get a real suspension. We got in-house suspension, where they just make us sit in the conference room all day and do bookwork from all of our classes. And it seems like the teachers really enjoy giving us bookwork too. Like they've just been waiting to give some student a heap of work to do that the rest of the class never sees.

We all know why they don't actually suspend us where we'll have to be absent from school—because South Bay High is known for all of its fancy accreditations. And having the least amount of student and faculty absences is a top priority here. So, unless you do something drastic, you won't get seriously sent home, not even for a day.

Well, Trecee did get kicked out, but she deserved it. That heffa came up here with the intent to create drama and we really don't need any more. Misty was in-house with us, but I doubt seriously that it'll affect her one way or another. She probably thinks of it as a damn vacation, knowing her. It's only the first week of school and already I'm looking forward to June. Enemies can do that to a sistah.

Do you know that broad Misty had the nerve to call me at Mama's and apologize for almost getting me killed? What the hell kind of apology can undo that? I would like to know. She is straight trippin' if she thinks I'm gone give her another chance to make amends. As many times as she's broken her word about starting mess, she's going to need stitches to repair it this time cause I could care less. I have had it with her crazy behind.

Believe it or not, she was shunned momentarily from South Central, by the Queen herself, Miss Shae. But, by the end of the day she had wormed her way back in by supplying some new dirt on this girl Tania. Shae can't stand Tania. So, the Misty drama continues, as usual.

I don't know what to do about KJ. Ever since all this drama with Trecee started, he has been trying to get back with me and I don't really mind, to tell you the truth. But, I also kinda like this cat Jeremy. OK, not kinda. I've been jocking Jeremy on the low for a while now. I ain't never dated no White boy before.

Jeremy and I have grown kinda tight in class this week. The two days I was there, before I was banned to the library, he sat next to me and wrote little notes on his notebook making fun of Mrs. Peterson. We've known each other for a while but we've never had a class together before. When I was sent to the library for the rest of the week he came to visit me every day during class when he was supposed to be going to the restroom. He's just so sweet.

Jeremy and I seem to have a lot in common. He listens to Southern style and East Coast rap, like me. He likes to read and just kick it, like me. He works hard, even though he doesn't have to. His parents are loaded. And, he's the finest boy in the entire school. Even with all of the bull of this week fresh in my head, I'm still looking forward to the weekend. If for no other reason, so I can put Drama High behind me for a couple of days.

~ 1 ~
Press 'n' Curl

*"Don't you ever worry about that
'Cause I don't mind being black"*

—SCHOOL DAZE SOUNDTRACK

My weekly hair routine is like a ritual. When Mama gets her hair done, she calls it a *"rogacion de cabeza"*: a cleansing of the head.

I love the way my hair looks and smells when it's pressed. I like to use Pantene and sometimes Thermasilk. My other tools include a Gold 'n' Hot blow-dryer and flat iron, two hot combs and an oven, five silver clips, a comb, a scrunchie and some Smooth as Silk hair spray. My girl Shawntrese's mom does hair and works for the guy who makes this spray. It's the bomb. It never crunches up and leaves white imprints on my hair when I flatten it.

I lightly press my edges before separating and pressing my hair. It's kinda pretty, the way it shines and smokes when I press it. It shimmers like ocean water in the afternoon sun. I'm basically frying my hair, but I still love the way it smells. Almost like sweet, burnt cantaloupe.

"Jayd, why do you press your hair when you know you just gone braid it up tomorrow, like some little thugette," my mom says, walking in the bathroom to get her manicure set. It's her night to do her nails, before her very social weekend officially begins.

My mom hates that her daughter wears cornrows in her

hair. She's ultra feminine and I can be too. But, I also like to wear baggy jeans and boxer shorts sometimes. It's just more comfortable to me. Same with my hair. It's cool to wear it out sometimes. But, truth be told, it's just easier to braid it up.

"Mom, now you know I can't be going to work with school hair. I got to be fresh for the weekend, just like you," I say, smiling at my mom, whose now holding her big Tupperware container full of nail stuff: cotton balls, polishes, polish remover, tissue, cuticle cream and clippers, nail files and buffers of all shapes and sizes, a stick-on design booklet, some lotion with a box of plastic wrap to make her feet extra soft, and baby oil for her pumice stone. Her heels are hella rough, just like mine.

"Jayd, me doing my hands and feet is totally different from you doing your hair." She takes her container into the living room, and dumps the contents onto the carpet. She comes back into the bathroom and fills the container with warm water and soap to soak her hands and feet in.

"You go through this entire three-hour production every Friday to wear it like some little dude on the street all week."

"Mom, lots of sistahs wear their hair in rows."

"Yeah, and they're all gay."

"Mom," I say, sounding shocked. She can be so stereotypical sometimes.

"So, you telling me Alicia Keys and Queen Latifah are gay?" I point out, while pressing the first layer of my hair. I start at the back of my neck and work my way up my head. I have to be careful not to burn my shoulders and chest. I use a thick washcloth under the hot comb while I pull it through my hair. If I do it right, I can get a little bump at the ends of my hair.

"I don't know about them other girls," my mom says while trying not to spill the water from her Tupperware container–turned–foot soaker on the carpet, "but you better not be. It's a wonder you got any little boys running around after you at all, especially KJ."

I almost burn myself as I pull the hot comb through my hair. "What do you mean by that?" That was more than a little insulting. My mom can stab a sistah when she wants to. I don't know why she gets like that, especially with me.

"Oh, Jayd, you can be so sensitive sometimes. All I'm saying is that dudes usually like sistahs that wear cute, girly stuff all the time. And girls who wear their hair like girls, not like Snoop Dogg."

"But, Mom, women in Africa have been wearing their hair like this since the beginning of time." As my mom rolls her eyes, slowly losing interest as she does any time I disagree with her, the phone rings.

"Hello-o," my mom says, almost cooing. "Oh, hey, baby. You know I'm doing my nails tonight. What's up?"

That must be her main dude, Ras Joe. He's a big, big dude with long dreads hanging down his back. He's hella light-skinned with them funny-colored eyes. And, he's got money. I don't know how he gets it, but he got it, and he loves spending it on my mom.

Maybe there's some truth to what my mom's saying. I've never had a dude buy me stuff like her before. Maybe if I showed a little leg on the regular, dudes would treat me more like a lady.

What am I saying? I sound like Misty now. Besides, all that glitters damn sure ain't gold. Ras Joe is cool, but he don't hang around all the time. My mother got to sit by the phone and wait for that fool to call. That ain't treating nobody like a lady, or even a friend for that matter.

I also think Ras Joe got a family at home, but I ain't sure. My mom don't tell me stuff like that. She talks to her girl-friends, who I call my aunties, about stuff like that. But, she ain't never been to his house, and I don't think she ever met none of his four kids.

"Baby, now, you know Friday night is my night to beautify

myself for the weekend. I am nowhere near ready for you tonight." I don't even know why she play like she ain't going out with him. She's already taking her feet out of the water and picking out polish.

"All right, baby. See you in a little while."

See, what'd I say? Now I'm gone have to speed up my pressing process to get out of her way. I know she's going to want to shower before polishing her nails. Pressing don't take too long and that's all I need the bathroom for. I can style my hair in her bedroom mirror.

I can't decide how to do my hair though. I want to put some cornrows in, but I'm too tired and I have to get up and go to work tomorrow morning. Granted, it ain't as early as 5:30 A.M. on school days, but 7:30 A.M. is still early to me.

"Don't slip up and get caught, 'cause I'm coming for that number-one spot." Ludacris is announcing a phone call from somebody right in the middle of my hair session. Everybody that knows me knows that Friday night is hair night. And, depending on if it's just a simple press and curl or something a little more sassy, it could take all night long.

"Hello."

"Hey, Jayd," says a male voice I don't recognize, but it kinda sounds familiar—and White. Who is this dude? Oh, it must be . . .

"It's Jeremy. What's up?"

"Hey, Jeremy," I say, sounding shocked as I don't know what.

"You sound surprised to hear from me. You didn't think I'd call you, huh?"

He got that right. With all that went down today with Trecee and KJ, I'd kinda forgot that I exchanged numbers with Jeremy in class the other day.

"Nah, actually I didn't. What's goin' on with ya?" I say, trying to sound like I'm happy to hear from him. But honestly, I just got my combs hot and I don't want them to burn.

"Did I catch you at a bad time? You sound a little busy." He sounds so cute when he's nervous.

"Well, Friday night is my hair night."

"You're doing your hair? I thought that's what girls said to get rid of guys they don't want to talk to," he says, sounding like he's half-smiling and half-serious.

"Not Black girls. Depending on what we're doing to our hair, it can be an all-night production," I say, taking the two pressing combs out of the oven. I use a white washcloth to set them on. If the imprint from the comb is black, it's too hot. But, if it's light–brown, the combs are just right to get my kinks straight. And, if there's no imprint, they're not hot enough, which means they should be returned to the oven immediately. Once my combs are hot, I like to keep them hot, just for the sake of consistency. Once the combs are allowed to cool, it changes the flow of the pressing session and the texture of my hair due to the minutes passed; it's almost like starting all over from scratch.

"So what you're saying is you really do have to do your hair and you can't talk to me now." God, he sounds so sexy over the phone.

"I can call you back a little later." I glance over at the radio to see what time it is.

"It's about 8:30 P.M. now. So, give me until about 9:30 or 10 o'clock and I'll be done," I say, touching my hot combs to the palm of my hand. They've cooled off completely now. And, my hair is not as poofy as it was when I first finished blow-drying it a half hour ago. I got to go.

"Well, actually, me and my friends are going to hang tonight. I wanted to know if you wanted to join us."

What! No plans. No warning. Uh-uh. A sistah got to finish her hair and get some rest. It's been a rough first week of school and I need to chill out. But, damn, I want to hang with him and his crew too. I want to get to know this boy. I got to be smooth, but not rude or desperate. And quick. My hair gets dirty from all this airplane pollution by my mom's house. The planes landing at LAX fly right over her building and I know they leave all kinds of particles in the air. Here comes one now.

"What the hell is that noise?" Jeremy asks.

"I'll tell you when it passes," I shout into the phone. You know folk that don't live near the airport don't understand. My mom's immune to it. She just automatically turns the TV up when she hears one coming. I'm kinda used to it as well. But it can get annoying, especially on the weekends. It seems like a plane passes about every ten seconds.

"That was a Boeing 747."

"Did it land in your backyard?"

"No. I don't have a backyard here."

"Where is here?" Jeremy says, sounding a little confused.

"I'm at my mom's house in Inglewood." Now I really have to go. My hair is cold, so are my combs, and the oven is baking. Electricity ain't free.

"Can I call you tomorrow?" I say, trying not to sound too hurried.

"Yeah, sure. Well, do you want to hang out tomorrow night or will you be doing your nails then?" Oh, I see he's going to be a funny one.

"So you got jokes, do you? Well, let's see how funny you are tomorrow night. I'll call you after I get off work."

"Work? What time will that be?"

"About six o'clock."

"All right, then. I'll see you tomorrow, Jayd."

"Have fun, Jeremy, and I'll give you a call tomorrow—nails done and all," I say, trying to be funny.

"Later funny girl."

I hang up my phone and put it on the counter next to the snag-a-tooth blow-dryer. The teeth in the comb attachment are always breaking on my Gold 'n' Hot.

I have a date with Jeremy the White boy tomorrow night. What am I going to wear? How should I do my hair? Well, I could row it. I mean, he must think it looks cool like that, right? Or should I wear it a little different, show him another side of Miss Jayd Jackson? I don't know. My mom got me wanting to change up my style now.

"Whatcha doin', man? I'm coming for that number-one spot." There's Luda again. Who's this now?

"Hello," I say, sounding hella irritated.

It's a private number. What's the point of caller ID if people can still block their numbers?

"Hey, girl. It's your daddy. Why you sound so snappy?" Why is he calling me this time of night? Usually by now he'd be asleep on his couch.

"Oh, hey, Daddy. I was just doin' my hair and the phone keeps ringing. Why are you calling so late?" It ain't like me and my daddy chat all that much, so something must be up.

"What are you doing the last weekend of next month?"

"I don't know. Working, I'm sure," I say, a little snide. He don't break me off no money. He gives my mom the court-mandated child support, which she then splits with Mama and Daddy, leaving nothing left over for me.

"Well, can you get the afternoon off that Sunday? We're having a little barbecue for your uncle William. He's moving back to Mississippi with his new wife and I want you to be there."

He's always trying to make me go to family stuff and I can't stand it. Them people don't like me or my mom. And they're afraid of Mama. The Jacksons are good, Southern Baptist folks. They have a fish fry every Friday night, play Dominoes, Bid-Wiz, and Spades every Saturday night, and go to church all day long on Sunday.

"Daddy, I can't miss work. I need the money, remember? Besides, Sundays are no good for me anyway. You know I got to go back to Mama's and get ready for school." He don't know nothing about my life.

"What if I pick you up from work and give you a ride back to your grandmother's on Sunday?" This must be big. He don't usually make me offers like that.

"Why you want me to go so bad? I barely know Uncle William, and I don't know his new wife. I didn't even know he wasn't with the first one anymore, to tell you the truth."

My mom's standing in the bathroom door, looking at me out the corner of her eyes like, "Hurry up and finish in the bathroom so I can get ready for my man." I better wrap this up without too much protesting. Family is family, as Mama says.

"Jayd, don't be difficult. Just come. You may have some fun. You could even invite your little girlfriends—what are their names?" he says, acting as if he really ever knew.

"You mean Nellie and Mickey?"

"Yeah, them girls. How's school going anyway? Didn't you start back this week?"

"Yes, Daddy, but I really gotta go finish my hair now. I'll talk to you later."

"So, will I see you in a few weeks?" he asks, not letting me off the hook.

"Yes, I guess so. Now, I need to finish my hair."

"Oh, yeah, and wear it pretty. Not in them thug braids you always have in your hair. You're such a pretty girl, Jayd, with good hair too. You need to take advantage of that and stop trying to be so hard all the time." Sometimes my dad says things, not even realizing how badly he makes me feel. My two parents alone are enough to warrant me a couple of episodes on Dr. Phil.

"Bye, Daddy."

"Bye, baby."

Now maybe I can finish my hair. I'm too tired to put any braids in it now, that's for sure. I guess I'll just go with a simple press and curl, and worry about the finishing touches tomorrow.

~ 2 ~
The Date

"You don't know my name."

—ALICIA KEYS

"Welcome to Simply Wholesome. What can I get for you?" I've been sweating the clock all day. It's almost time for me to get off and all I can think about is my date tonight with Jeremy.

"May I have the spinach enchiladas, a small green salad, hold the sprouts, with a wheat germ and ginger root smoothie?" She's going to be on the toilet all night long.

"That will be $13.85." I can't believe how high the prices are here. Man, if I didn't work here I don't know how I'd be able to eat this food.

"I know it's some soldiers in here. Where they at?" There's Destiny's Child again announcing yet another text message from KJ.

"Jayd, please call me so we can talk about this whole Trecee thing. I want to put it behind us and get back to us. Love, Your Man."

If he only knew that I got a new man to kick it with now. I can't wait to get off of work and call Jeremy. I've been looking forward to it since last night. I couldn't even sleep, I was so excited. And, I can always get my sleep on.

Should I text message this fool back? Nah. Let him sweat, like he's been doing since yesterday.

For real though. Last weekend I didn't have a man at all. KJ broke up with me and I was dreading going back to school. Now, I got two dudes on my jock and the first week of school is over. Life just keeps on going.

Speaking of which, it's time for me to roll. I can call Jeremy while I'm waiting at the bus stop. I would ask my mom to pick me up, but I know she's still asleep from her late night. She walked in the door as I was leaving for work this morning.

"Later y'all. See you in the morning," I say to no one in particular. Everybody around here is real laid back.

"All right, Jayd. You take it easy." Shahid always speaks to me, even if he's in the middle of taking a customer's order.

I walk out the side door and down the stairs, which take me right across the street from the bus stop. It's another hot, sunny day in L.A. and the people are out. The cars are shining, the sun is gleaming. The smoke from the buses and beat-up cars passing by mixed with the L.A. smog is enough to make me drop dead of lung cancer right here on the street.

Most of the bus stops around here, just like in Compton, don't have pretty little benches and covered spots like in the South Bay. So, I just need to find a place to lean so I can call this cat and see what's crackin' for tonight.

I saved his number in my phone last night and gave him a special ring.

"Hello," says a woman's voice. It must be his mom. This boy gave me his home phone number? That's rare nowadays.

"Hi. Is Jeremy home?" I ask, trying to sound all sweet and innocent, like I ain't jockin' her son.

"Yes. May I tell him who's calling, please?" Wow. So proper and all. If somebody calls for me at my mom's or Mama's they usually get a rude grunt followed by a loud-ass "Jaaaaaaayd! Pick up the phone." Thus, the evolution of my cell.

"Yes. This is Jayd."

"Hold on while I get him for you, Jayd," she says, with a deep, Southern drawl. It almost sounds like Mama's.

"Sammy, tell your brother to pick up the line. He has a call from Jayd," I hear her say to one of Jeremy's brothers.

"Hey, Jayd. How was work?" He sounds even yummier than he did last night.

"Work was cool, thanks for asking."

"So, your hair and everything's all done? No more excuses for not hangin' out with me?"

"Oh, you've got more jokes, I see? So, what did you have in mind?"

"Well, I was thinking we could go to the movies and just hang out at the pier afterward. Do you have a curfew?"

At Mama's I can't even really go out. But if I do, I know to be home before 11 P.M.; no question. It's always been like that for the girls. The boys, on the other hand, have no curfew. Look at Bryan. He may come home, he may not. Let me try something like that. They'll be talking about my ass-whipping for years to come.

"Well, I'm over my mom's house, so as long as I get home before she does, it's all good. And, she usually hangs out pretty late."

"Cool. So, what time do you want me to pick you up? The evening flicks start at around 8 P.M."

"It's 6 P.M. now. By the time I get home, shower, dress, and do something to my hair, which is already flat, it will be at least 8 P.M."

"Let's say 8 P.M., then."

"All right. You want to give me directions now or call me later?" He's so polite. Good home training.

"I'm just chillin,' waiting for the bus to come. So, I can give them to you now if you're ready. Where are you coming from?"

"I'm in P.V. You said you're in Inglewood, right?"

Damn. He lives in Palos Verdes. His parents must be ballers, for real. That's where all the hellafied rich folk live. I heard Johnnie Cochran got a house out there.

"Yeah, Inglewood. You know where the Forum is?"

"Yeah, where the Lakers used to play, right?"

"Exactly. That street is Prairie. Take Prairie till you get to Arbor Vitae, make a left. Go down to LaBrea Drive and I'm in the first apartment building on the left, #7."

"Do I have to dial a code at the gate or anything?" He's so cute. None of these apartments around here have security gates.

"No, baby. Just come on up and knock on the door. See you at 8 P.M. By the way, how should I dress?"

"I don't know. However you want to I guess. I've never had a girl ask me that before. Just be yourself."

Myself. Well, which self should I be? The little roughneck Jayd, the Dashiki-wearing Jayd, or the laid-back jeans and a cute top from Baby Phat Jayd. Yeah, that Jayd is the one going out with Jeremy tonight.

"All right, then. I'll see you soon, Jeremy."

"Bye, Jayd."

So, he wants to go to the movies and walk on the pier. Which pier, I wonder? He must be talking about Redondo. I know it's gonna get cold no matter where we end up, so I better take my jacket too. What am I going to wear? And, what about my hair? It's so flat now. But, after ten minutes by the beach, I'll look like a troll doll.

I decide to touch up my press and just let it lay back in a tight ponytail on the right side of my neck. I'm wearing my cute capri jeans from Lerner's and my pink and white Baby Phat tank with my Baby Phat flip-flops. I gotta downscale the diva in me a little. I don't want to overdress for the beach crowd.

Usually when I would go out with KJ, he would give me explicit details of what to wear and how to wear my hair. I was there to accentuate his outfit, basically an accessory. It's kinda cool just wearing what I feel like and not worrying about anyone saying anything about my toes hangin' out at night.

As I go to the living room closet to get my jacket, I hear a knock at the door.

"Who is it?"

"It's Jeremy. I'm here to pick up Jayd."

Oh no, this dude is early. This I'm not used to. I still have to put on my perfume, check my nose for buggas one more time and say a little prayer that I don't embarrass myself in front of his fine ass.

"Just a minute, Jeremy. I'll be right there." I quickly spray on some Escada Rockin' Rio and dab a little Egyptian musk oil behind my ears. My mom swears it drives Ras Joe out of his mind. I check everything else and say a quick prayer before running out the door.

My mom's still in her room, recouping for tonight's adventures I'm sure. I leave her a note on the fridge telling her where I'll be and with whom.

I open the door and there he is, looking as good as he smells. "Hey, Jeremy. Sorry to keep you waiting." He's wearing some typical White boy South High gear. Levi's that are hella worn-out, loose fitting, but not too baggy, a T-shirt, a baseball hat with the rim folded real tight, and some brown, suede Birkenstocks on his feet. This cat is straight outta P.V.

"Hey, Jayd." He looks at my straight hair, my big gold hoops hangin' off my ears, my jeans, and finally, my feet. I've always been self-conscious about two things: my breasts and my feet. I took care of my overly large breasts last year, but I think I'm stuck with my feet for life.

"You look cute in sandals. Ready to go?" I don't know if he's joking or not, but I ain't gonna compromise the one and only compliment I've ever received on my feet.

"Thank you. Yeah, I'm ready. Will I fit in with your crowd, or is the jacket too much?"

"Jayd, you never struck me as the type who cares about what people think," he says to me as I turn around to lock the door behind us.

"Damn, how many locks you got?" My mom has four bolts on her door. She's been robbed a couple of times, so she's not playin' anymore. Now she just gotta worry about getting in the door in time if she's running from somebody.

"I know. My mom's a bit paranoid."

"Is she here? Does she want to meet the White guy taking her daughter out?" he asks, only half-joking. He has the most beautiful smile. It's like his extra-curly eyelashes just light up when he smiles. And his teeth are perfect.

"Did you have braces?"

"Where the hell did that come from?" he says, still smiling. "Yes, I did, now answer my question. Does your mom want to meet me?" How do I tell him my mom's tired out from her date last night, and conserving her energy for her date to-night without making her look bad?

"She does, but she's got cramps. She said to tell you to be careful with her baby. So, be careful with me."

Jeremy takes my hand and leads me down the narrow stairway to the front where his car's parked. What a sweet ride. His car is notorious around South Bay High. It's a powder blue '65 Mustang convertible with a cream-colored leather interior. The original wood paneling is perfect. It's the nicest car I've ever been in.

"What did you do to get this car?" I say, knowing that his dad's an engineer with eighteen U.S. patents, so far. That's also notorious knowledge around school.

"Actually, it's kinda the family first car. Both my older brothers drove this car until they went off to college. Now, I get to drive it until I go to college."

He opens the door for me and I slide into the leather seat. It smells like leather polish. Everything's shining like he just got it washed.

"You mind if the top is down? Or is it too much wind on you?"

"Nah, I'm cool." Good thing I wore my hair back.

"I thought maybe we could skip the movie and just kinda hang out. It's a nice night and I want to be outside. And, I want to talk to you, and we can't do that in the movies."

We end up in Manhattan Beach by the pier. It's a cool little spot. There are bookstores, trendy little clothing stores with stuff I could never afford, and coffeehouses. My favorite coffee spot is right on the corner, The Coffee Bean & Tea Leaf.

"You mind if we stop here? I want to get a café vanilla."

"Yeah, I like Coffee Bean too. I usually get the chocolate ice blended."

"Well, aren't we just the exact opposite of each other?" I say, while at the same time eyeing the joint to see if there are any other Black people in the spot. Nope, not a one.

"You wanna sit down in here? I'll get our drinks, you can find a table." He's such a gentleman. If I was with KJ, I'd be paying for my own coffee, since he's not into the whole coffee shop thing. And we definitely wouldn't be sitting down and talking up in this place.

After Jeremy comes back with our drinks, we talk until the place closes. I find out he's a true surfer dude. He wakes up at 4 A.M. to get out and surf every morning. His mother's from South Carolina, his dad's from Brooklyn. His mom's a Baptist, his dad is Jewish, he and his brothers don't know what to believe and don't really care. He's the baby of the three of them. They have a dog, Ganymede, that doesn't bark.

"I've never heard of a dog that doesn't bark. Are you sure she's not broken or something?" I say, sipping the last of my drink.

"No, she's not broken. She's a basenji."

"A what?" I ask.

"A basenji, or better known as the African barkless dog," he says, sounding very proud.

"Now I know you're lying. Ain't nothing in Africa quiet, especially not a dog. What's the point of having a dog that doesn't bark?" I say. If it weren't for the dogs and the helicopters, we would probably be able to hear crickets at night, like in other neighborhoods.

"Well, I'm not getting into the history of Ganymede's ancestors, but my mom specifically chose her because she doesn't bark." Now, that's strange. Usually people get dogs to warn them of danger, which they do by barking. So, why wouldn't she want a dog that barks?

"Okay, Jeremy, whatever. What about the name Ganymede? Where did that come from?"

"Actually, I named her after one of the moons of Jupiter. It's my favorite planet." He pulls up his right sleeve to reveal a tattoo of Jupiter on his arm. Jeremy's hella smart, but doesn't flaunt it. I really like that about him and everything else so far. When the staff tells us they're closing, I think the date might be over.

"Well, I'm glad I got to know more about you. And, thank you for the coffee. I had a really good time."

"Are you trying to get rid of me or something? It's only midnight and the car doesn't turn back into a pumpkin until 2 A.M. Care to see it happen?" Damn, he's sexy when he's being a smart-ass.

"You know what, you don't have to be funny. I just assumed that since the place closed down we were going home."

"Why would you assume that? The night is young. I want you to meet some of my friends outside of school, if you're up for it."

Oh, hell, where's he taking me? You know how all them movies end with the little Black girl being sacrificed or some craziness like that. But, I'm gone risk it 'cause I really don't want the night to end just yet.

We get back in his car and cruise down P.C.H. toward P.V. It's a perfect night to be by the beach. The moon is full, the sky is clear, and the air is chilly, but not too cold. As if he read my mind, Jeremy reaches back into the backseat and grabs his poncho pullover, a surfer must-have, and hands it to me.

"Here. I know it can get a bit cool, especially for people who aren't used to cold beach nights."

He's damn right about that. This cute little jacket I brought ain't doing a damn thing to keep me warm. This poncho looks like it's just what I need. And, so does he.

"Thank you, 'cause a sistah is getting hella cold," I say, pulling the poncho over my head, careful not to mess up my already poofy hair.

"Why'd you do that?"

"Do what?" I say, hella self-conscious.

"Try not to touch your hair. The poncho won't hurt it, you know."

"Oh no, but it will. You see what the ocean air has already done to it? I don't want your friends to see me looking like a madwoman."

"Your hair is really important to you, isn't it?"

"You just don't get it, do you? My hair is very sensitive to the elements. The slightest change in air temperature, moisture, or something as simple as putting on a poncho can permanently affect the style of hair for the night."

"Well, I think your hair looks sexy like it is. Besides, you look way better than any of the people you're going to meet tonight." This dude is really diggin' me, ain't he?

"Here we are." We pull up to what to me looks like nowhere. Or rather, a deserted beach where they sacrifice people. He parks the car on the sand, grabs my hand, and leads me down a steep sand hill. At the bottom of the hill, right off the beach, you can see a bonfire and smell marijuana burning in the wind.

As we get closer, I can hear drumming and someone strumming a guitar. People are just lying around, kickin' it. Most of them look high off something, the rest look like they're mesmerized by the motion of the waves.

"Jayd, meet my surfing crew. Crew, this is Jayd."

They look at me, nod a cool "What's up?" and go back to their individual trances.

"So, what do you think?" Jeremy asks as he leads me to sit down on the sand next to him.

"Honestly, this is the most peaceful I've been in a long time. All night I haven't thought about the drama of this past week at all. Thank you for taking me out. I'm having a good time."

"Well, I hope it won't be the last." Jeremy pulls me in close to him and wraps me in his arms. He smells like vanilla incense and Polo cologne. It's at this moment I realize I could easily fall in love with him. I've got to call Nellie in the morning and tell her all about our night.

I purposely turned off my phone when we left the house because KJ has been on my jock all weekend. I didn't want anything to ruin our night, especially not any annoying phone calls or text messages. And, it's perfect. I can't wait to go home tomorrow night and tell Mama all about our date.